Spectacle

Also by Susan Steinberg

Hydroplane
The End of Free Love

Spectacle

STORIES

Susan Steinberg

Graywolf Press

Stories from the collection first appeared, in earlier forms, in the following literary journals:
"Cowboys" and "Signifier" in *American Short Fiction.*
"Cowgirl," "Signified," and "Spectacle" in *Conjunctions.*
"Superstar" in *Pleiades.*
"Universe" in *Web Conjunctions.*
"Spectator" in *Western Humanities Review.*
"Cowgirl" also appeared in *Pushcart Prize XXXVI: Best of the Small Presses.*

This publication is made possible, in part, by the voters of Minnesota through a Minnesota State Arts Board Operating Support grant, thanks to a legislative appropriation from the arts and cultural heritage fund, and through a grant from the National Endowment for the Arts. Significant support has also been provided by Target, the McKnight Foundation, Amazon.com, and other generous contributions from foundations, corporations, and individuals. To these organizations and individuals we offer our heartfelt thanks.

ART WORKS.
arts.gov

MINNESOTA
STATE ARTS BOARD

CLEAN
WATER
LAND &
LEGACY
AMENDMENT

TARGET.

Published by Graywolf Press
250 Third Avenue North, Suite 600
Minneapolis, Minnesota 55401

All rights reserved.

www.graywolfpress.org

Published in the United States of America

ISBN 978-1-55597-631-6

2 4 6 8 9 7 5 3 1
First Graywolf Printing, 2013

Library of Congress Control Number: 2012949113

Cover design: Kyle G. Hunter

Cover photo: Mel Stuart / Westend61 / Getty Images

Contents

Spectacle

SUPERSTAR

I once hung out with this shit group of kids and they were just such shit.

This to say I made some mistakes.

Like breaking into this one guy's car.

Like stealing the stereo out of that car.

I was young and I didn't steal the stereo because I wanted the stereo.

I stole it, rather, because I wanted the guy.

This to say I just wanted some thing the guy owned.

This more to say that nothing else mattered in that moment except this thing the guy owned, this thing that, I now know, was not the guy.

Anyway there was nothing else in the car.

Had there been a jacket I would have stolen it.

Had anything else jarred loose—a mirror, an ashtray—I would have stolen that too.

But the stereo was the only thing I could snap out of its hole.

And so there I was, drunk and standing on the sidewalk at two a.m., the bar closing, the drunks stumbling out, holding a car stereo with both hands, a kind of person I didn't even know I could be, and my friends said, Run.

This to say I made a mistake.

Not because I got caught, because I did not get caught.

Because no one ever once got caught.

Because this was Baltimore.

And if you know the place, you know what I mean.

If you know the place, you're likely from there.

I mean you're likely still there.

Which I no longer am.

Which doesn't mean I figured it out.

It only means a window appeared and I went through the window before it disappeared.

Metaphorically I mean.

But it's not time for anything deep.

We're just talking about this mistake I made.

How I can't make myself feel better.

Because I'm awake and thinking the thoughts I think at four a.m.

Me, some guy, and it's always the same.

Me, some guy, and we're lying around a bed like kids.

Then one thing, another, his hands on my face, his face near my face, and just before it all starts up, I'm yanking a stereo out from its hole.

I'm backing out ass first from the car.

My friends are screaming, Run.

To say I shouldn't have stolen.

But I'd fallen hard for the guy whose stereo it was.

And when I fall hard, I fall like the proverbial ton of whatever, and by *fall* I mean I splinter everything around me.

Another might call it *apocalyptic*.

By *another,* I might mean the guy himself, the victim I mean, the guy headed away from me fast.

He might use the word *apocalyptic* when cracks form in the asphalt, when windows shatter, when women cover their daughters' eyes.

When he floats upward to heaven.

I'm not being melodramatic.

You've never been there to see it.

And this time, like every time, the entire world had splintered.

And because he'd been all night in the bar talking to some girl, I was splintering within this splintered world.

It was very complex.

The strategy I mean.

Like if he stood there, I stood here.

If he looked at me, I looked away.

And on and on and on.

God.

It was summer and it was a hundred degrees.

This is not an excuse but I'm just saying.

It was a hundred degrees and my friends said, Run, and we all ran up the street to my car, all of us too drunk to drive.

And six of us kids squeezed into the car, two up front, four in back, and somehow I ended up in the back, even though it was my car.

Somehow I ended up sitting on some guy's lap, the stereo on top of mine.

And somehow one of the guys ended up in the driver's seat, and he started the car and drove closer to the car I stole the stereo from, and we sat there.

And the radio, meaning the piece of shit radio in my car, was playing something from that summer, and the kids up front were singing, and there I was in the back of my car, some guy I didn't like gripping my hips.

I didn't know then what we were waiting for, sitting there outside the bar.

We were waiting for the guy whose stereo I stole to walk out.

We were waiting for the guy whose stereo I stole to get into his car and see that his stereo was gone.

But then what.

I mean what were we going to do about it.

That was the thing.

I had the stereo, but now what.

We'd hooked up, me and the guy whose stereo I stole, in the front of his car, the week before I stole the stereo and the week before that.

And the liquor, those nights, was doing its thing.

The stereo was doing its.

And the guy did this thing those nights where he tilted his head too far to one side when he moved in toward me.

There was something about this.

Nothing new.

That brilliant spinning in one's gut that no one knows how to describe.

That everything inside inching up and up, and this is why I wanted him.

And by *wanted* I mean I wanted to own him completely.

I wasn't dumb.

I knew that stealing a stereo was not the way to own a guy.

I knew that the way to own a guy was to push something down, push something else out.

I know that the way to own a guy, still, years later, is this.

Like recently, there was this incident.

There was this guy whose car I scraped by mistake with my car.

It was raining that day, a downpour, and the guy whose car I scraped by mistake was big and standing on the sidewalk, holding his sagging bags of groceries.

He was waiting for me to move my car so that he could get into his.

I mean I'd parked so close, he couldn't get into his car, and he was waiting in the downpour, burdened with his sagging bags, annoyed.

And when I backed up my car, one hand up, giving the obligatory wave, the obligatory thanks for waiting, I scraped his car with my side mirror, because of my shit parking job, and I heard it scrape, even through the sound of the radio, even through the rain and the windshield wipers' squeak.

And before I shut off the car, and before the rain refilled the windshield, I saw the guy drop his bags of groceries to the wet ground and smack his forehead with both hands.

I knew I had a choice to make.

And I knew the right choice was to get out of the car.

And I knew I had another choice to make.

And I knew the right choice was to be a guy.

As the rain refilled the windshield, I knew I had to open the door.

And as I opened the door, I heard first the downpour, then heard the guy calling me certain names reserved for women, certain names I'd been called before and would be called again, certain names I'd, eventually, later, not too much later, call others.

And as I stepped out of the car I was suddenly some very small thing, by which I mean I was suddenly a woman to this guy, absorbing these names reserved for women, standing there in the downpour, reduced to something snail small and just as tightly coiled.

I wanted to be a guy.

I wanted to be a certain type of guy.

But instead I said, Stop yelling at me.

And he said, Stop being a fucking whore.

And what does one say to that.

I wanted to say a lot of things.

I wanted to say, Is that the best you can do.

Because it was raining and we were standing in it and it didn't look like it would stop.

And his groceries might have slid, at any point, from the bottoms of their sagging bags.

The world could have come, is what I mean, at any point, to the standstill we'd been waiting for.

It would have been apocalyptic.

And this would have been his finale.

Whore.

But the point is not this.

The point is I wanted to be a guy.

By which I mean I wanted to get up in his face.

I'm not talking about anything deep.

I'm talking about a generic performance of guy.

I'm talking about strapping on the proverbial pair.

But I never had to.

Because there was this second guy walking down the sidewalk.

And this is the point.

This second guy was walking down the sidewalk and the second guy had seen the whole thing, had seen me scrape this first guy's car, had seen the first guy smack his head and yell at me, and the second guy walked up to the first guy and called the first guy an asshole.

And the second guy got up in the first guy's face and told the first guy to get back into his car, said there wasn't even a scratch, said, I'll call the cops if you do not get the fuck back into your car right now.

And the second guy asked me if I was okay.

And the second guy called me certain names reserved for women, certain other names I'd been called before and would be called again.

It was then I became some sweet thing.

It was then I pushed something down, pushed something else out.

It was then I knew I owned the situation, meaning I knew I now owned both guys.

It's not something I want to explain.

If you've got the parts you understand.

As for the rest of you.

Just know I knew it was good to be a woman.

Meaning it was very bad to be a woman.

And the first guy squeezed into his car and left.

And the rain slowed.

And the sun, at some point, came out.

Listen.

There's a chair across the room and were you here with me now, sitting in the chair across the room, I would get out of bed, I would walk across the room to the chair, I would sit at your feet, my head in your lap, my head demanding you pet it.

And you would pet it how I wanted it.

And bricks would loosen from the walls.

And sidewalks would fissure.

Animals would run to their dark holes filled with leaves.

I'm just saying.

Would I own you.

Do you think I would.

I'm just saying something.

I'm just saying I'm kind of a whore.

Which is not to say don't like me.

Because I'm also kind of sweet.

Which is just to say.

The world should no longer be about wanting and wanting the way it was when I was younger and dumber, drawing in my bed, drawing some asshole's name on my hand, and hearts.

But here we all are.

Meaning here I am wanting again.

The utter inconvenience of what I am.

The utter inconvenience of it all.

But I was just so fucking powerful that night.

I was in the backseat of my car that night.

I had a stolen stereo on my lap.

I was feeling like a superstar.

The kids up front were singing again.

And the bar door opened and the guy whose stereo I stole stumbled out.

Someone turned down the radio.

Someone was laughing, then everyone was laughing, even I was laughing my head off.

And the guy whose stereo I stole stumbled out with that girl on his arm, the girl stopping to untwist the strap on her shoe.

One of the kids up front said, Who's she, and my legs were shaking, then I wasn't laughing, and I almost screamed out the window, I've got your stereo, you dumb fuck.

I almost waved the stereo around, almost smashed it to the street right there in front of the bar, in front of the guy and the girl, and I would have screamed something, would have done all of this, but the guy driving my car sped off before I could scream.

Next someone turned up the radio and some song was on, and the six of us were riding up some burned-out Baltimore street.

There was no one on the street but us.

We were screaming out the words to this song.

Then another song came on and we knew that song too.

And it was only us, the six of us, singing on this crazy, burned-out Baltimore street.

I was just so fucking powerful in that moment.

Like how I'm just so fucking powerful in this moment.

Like how I kind of, admit it, own you.

I don't.

I mean I kind of, admit it, have you.

No.

I mean I think this is the climax.

This is it.

This is it now.

I rolled down the window and pushed my body, hands first, arms next, head next, upward through that open space and threw the stereo as hard as I could.

I heard it smash to bits against the side of some burned-out building.

I think you saw this coming.

I think you think, Big deal.

But someone could have gotten hurt.

I could have gotten caught.

It's enough that I feel like shit.

Because I would have done almost anything that night.

Though I resisted hard at first.

Not stealing the stereo, which I didn't resist.

I mean something about the guy whose lap I was on.

He pulled me back into the car like a savior.

He whispered to me to spend the night.

I said, No way.

And he said, Why not.

And I said, Because.

And he said, That's not an answer.

And I said, It's the only answer you're getting.

But later that night, when it was me and him on some sidewalk somewhere, he came closer, nearly tilting his head, and I closed my eyes, pretended.

There are things that now I know.

Nothing deep.

Like that only the guy is the guy.

Like that objects are only objects.

Listen to me.

It had been a hundred degrees that day, and it was a hundred degrees that night, and after the guy and I hooked up, we were lying on top of his sheet, sticking to his sheet, a fan droning on the tilted dresser.

And I was already looking at the door, I was already thinking of moving like a ghost toward the door, I was already thinking of moving like a ghost away from that burned-out city, and I was praying for the apocalypse, I was praying for that final standstill, and when the standstill came, I moved.

It wasn't the real standstill, of course, but a tease.

Still, it felt real.

Still, it lit the proverbial match.

It looked like a window and I went through it and landed here.

All this to say I've learned a few things.

All this to say I will not steal your things.

All this to say if I did steal your things, I know now the things will not have your name.

And they will not have your eyes.

And they will not smell like your sweat forever.

And they will not make me remember your hands on my face.

Or what song was playing when you tilted your head.

Or the lie you said that I believed.

They will only make me remember the sound the stereo made when it hit the burned-out building.

A sound I can't describe.

A sound that was more like a color.

A color that was more like a pain.

A pain that was more like an answer.

UNDERFED

; there was the time I stood outside; it had snowed the night
before; a sound in the distance could have been voices; it could
have been something else; it could have been machinery; it
could have been just in my head; I wanted the sound to be something else: waves crashing to the sand, an ocean I was standing
in, an ocean I was drowning in; I wanted to be sinking into
sand; but I was standing in snow under a tree; I was standing in
my underthings; there was something about just standing there
like that; there was something about just standing still, the sky
about to turn light; I was not in a state of dire need; but I'd been
up late thinking of dire things; I'd been thinking, for instance,
of the reasons girls love love; I'd been thinking, as well, of the
reasons guys love war; I every day bought the paper from the
box on the corner; I every day spread the paper across my bed; I
was reading up on various wars; I followed wars in various places
I didn't know; I was becoming well informed on battle; I was
becoming well informed on invasion; because there was nothing
going on where I was at all; there was nothing going on where I
was but snow; everyone had gone away for the winter; everyone
loved to leave for the winter; and yes, I was feeling abandoned;

yes, I was feeling melodramatic; then this one friend called who hadn't yet left; and of course he would leave for the winter too; he would leave, of course, like everyone else; but I wasn't yet thinking of him leaving; and that night I was up to nothing; I was all the time up to my ears in nothing; and so he called and it wasn't my fault he called; and so it was completely his fault; look: I want to make a public confession; I want an interrogation; I want a fitting punishment; and where was I on that winter night: I was with this guy in a bar; and who else was with us on that night: there was no one else but us; and did I know that night he had a girlfriend: yes, I knew he had a girlfriend, but I knew nothing specific about his girlfriend, she was just a cutout of a girlfriend, she was just a flattened thing; and how did I feel about this: I felt all right, I felt pretty good, I felt pretty great; so punish me however you see fit; but know I wasn't all bad; in the bar that night I knew to get this body out the door; so I got this body up the street; I got this body up the stairs and laid it flat on the bed; I was home, safe; I was where I belonged; and I'm sorry my thoughts turned dire; I'm sorry I'd been reading up on wars; I'm sorry for the metaphor; but I confess I was thinking of battle; I confess I was thinking invasion; I knew too much about crossing lines; then I was rushing outside to think in the cold; I can't explain; years before, things with me seemed all right; I was with this nice guy back then; all my friends liked this guy; he would pick me up in his car; he would take me on hikes; he owned things for going on hikes; I didn't know the proper names of the things he owned; I still, years later, don't know their proper names; they clamped to things and heated up and stuck through ice and stuck through mud; the guy and I would walk up hills; we would sleep on wet grass; we would stand there holding hands, staring at some or another sunset; and I would pretend to like the sunset; I would pretend to be a better person than I was; but I would stare at the sunset thinking things like: Tragic, like: Big fucking deal, like: This is not meant to be; it was not, me and him, meant to be; I said, This is not meant to be, on the ride home from our final hike; the radio was up too high; I said, Did you hear me; he pointed to an ear, said, I can't hear you; then his hand was somewhere on me; I said, This is not meant to be; I said, I'm incapable of falling for you; I said, I'm incapable of falling in love; I'm a wreck, I said; I need another wreck, I said; It's my father, I said, of course; It's my mother, I said, of course; I turned down the radio; I said, Did you hear me; he kept on driving; I turned up the radio; I will wreck you, I said; I swear, I said; I was talking at the radio; I was talking at the heat vent; I was talking at my dirty knees; I'd hiked all day through mud; I was scraped all over, dirty all over; I wasn't averse to dirt; I was averse to something else: like the pressure of having to pretend I cared about a bird, a stone, a star: like the pressure of having to be so fucking nice: like the pressure of having to be a certain type of guy when I was just a certain type of girl; I was just two tits a hole and a heartbeat; I'd heard that somewhere, my brother, my father; I'd heard this somewhere too: two tits a slit and a heartbeat; that was this body; and this body was standing in the snow; this body was up to its ears in nothing; this body was thinking of invasion; this body could be a wrecking ball; this body could swing right in and wreck your home; I confess: it could make itself do awful things; it had done plenty of awful plenty of times; just look at it up in that old tree as a kid; just look at it dangling upside down from the highest branch that could hold it; just look at it dangling by its legs; this was a family trip to the South; this was the trip I learned to climb a tree; and it was on this trip I learned to dive through waves; we stayed in a cottage by the beach; my brother threw bread to birds; my father sat on the sand; my mother slept in the cottage; there was always the sound of waves; I know it all sounds spectacular; and I assure you some moments were; but I assure you some moments were not; nights, I stayed in the tree well after my name had been called; I wasn't hungry for dinner; I wasn't ever hungry; I was underfed and happy being underfed; I dangled, nights, from the highest branch; I waited for my father to come back from the bar; I waited for my father to walk under the tree; from up in the tree I would see him stumble up the sidewalk, shirt untucked; I would see him drop his keys to the grass, hear him cuss, see him stoop to the grass; and on one night I would drop down from the tree; and on this night I would crush my father to dust; because I knew it was my job to crush him; because I was the only daughter of the man; because he was the man and I was the only daughter; but most nights my father walked up the sidewalk; he walked into the cottage; the screen door slammed; the cottage went dark; and eventually I would come down from the tree; I would lie on the grass; I would consider stars; I would consider my size; I would consider how the world began; it began, as you know, as a spark; and I began, as well, as a spark; and then everything grew; and a lot of things happened; and a lot more things happened; and the future was the present; and the present was a battle in my head; it was another line for me to cross; and no, I wasn't terribly cold; and no, the sound wasn't what I thought it was; it wasn't what I wanted it to be; it wasn't waves crashing onto a beach; and yes, I wanted something to come through the snow; yes, I wanted the savior to come through the snow; and yes, one day the savior would come through the snow; but no, it wasn't on that day; on that day, I was still unsaved; on that day,

I was waiting to be punished for my sins; so punish me however you see fit; I shouldn't have gone with the guy to the bar; we were not supposed to be in the bar; he was supposed to be with his girlfriend; I was supposed to be a better person than I was; I was supposed to be just about as regular a girl as I could be; but just look at us drinking way too much; just look at him looking at me like that; just look at him forgetting his girlfriend; we probably fell in love right there; it was probably total love right then; I was probably totally capable now of falling in love; on our last hike, the guy and I watched a bird soaring over a field; it was a hawk I think, and I wish I'd cared about that bird; and I wish I'd cared about that guy; but I dropped his hand; I sat on a rock; I watched him watch the bird; I'm sure he wasn't thinking the awful thoughts I was thinking; I'm sure he was only thinking of this bird moving through the space through which he was also moving; I'm sure he was feeling connected to it in a way I could not feel connected; but it was beautiful, I confess, the bird; it was spectacular, I confess; So am I awful, I asked the guy at the bar, and I can't remember why I asked; I knew he didn't think I was awful; because he was looking at me a certain way; because he was looking at me like he wanted to devour me; and I wanted, of course, to be devoured; and there was his hand; and there it was on me; and it felt, in that moment, like the world had ended; but the world hadn't ended just because it felt like it had; and so I downed my drink; I looked away; and the door was still there; and the street was still there; and the world was there beyond that; and walking home, I was feeling okay; and I was feeling okay because I was drunk; and I was feeling okay because I knew how to get this drunk body home; and I was feeling okay until a guy pushed a cart into my legs and said, I'll give you a thousand dollars to spend the night in your bed;

he was filthy; his clothes were torn; his cart was filled with trash; I said, You don't have a thousand dollars; I said, You don't even have a dollar; I kicked his cart; and I didn't mean to kick his cart so hard; then the snow began; and it would snow all night; look: it started out well enough, this spark; on our family trip to the South I met a girl; her name was two names pressed together, one a girl's and one a guy's; she was missing her front teeth; she said y'all; and she was the one who taught me how to climb a tree; she was the one who taught me how to dive through waves; climbing a tree was easy; I could climb a tree in seconds; I was scared, however, to dive through waves; there was something about the force; there was something about a force coming at me; there was something about the trust; but still I wanted to try; and so I stood one day in the ocean; and my brother was there, and the girl was there; and my father and her mother stood on the shore; my father and her mother were ankle-deep; I screamed to them, Watch me, but my father didn't look up; my brother screamed to them, Watch this, but my father was fooling with her mother's bathing-suit tie; her mother was kicking water at my father; my mother was back at the cottage pretending to sleep; my mother was back at the cottage staring at her hands; my mother was back at the cottage pulling hairs out from her head; I screamed to them, Watch me, as the biggest wave came rushing up, and the girl screamed, Go, y'all; and my brother and I both dove into the wave; and I could have drowned, you know; I would have drowned, you know; and did I want to drown; well, I didn't, you know; I just dove, felt cold, felt the tug of the world, emerged; I saw my father and her mother in the waterblurred distance; I heard my brother choking beside me; and no, I wasn't going ashore; I wasn't tired; I wasn't hungry; I wasn't cold; I wanted to stay in the water forever; I wanted to travel farther and farther out; farther out in the water, I could hear only water; I couldn't hear the girl's mother laughing; I couldn't hear my brother choking; I couldn't see my father looming how he often loomed; farther out was a world I could be in forever; so no, I wasn't going back; so I floated away, an abandoned boat; I floated, an abandoned shell; but then I felt my father's arms around me; and then I was screaming, No, and, No; and the girl's mother had no right laughing as my father dragged me from the water; and the girl had no right laughing; and my brother, my poor brother; and later that night my father went out; my mother slept in a chair; I climbed the tree outside the cottage; I dangled from the highest branch; and the sun went down; and the cottage went dead; and the blood rushed to my skull; and so what if I crushed him; I would put an end to something awful; I would be my brother's savior; I would be my mother's savior; and so I dangled from the branch; and the grass grew below my head; and day spread across the roots; and my father never walked up the sidewalk; and there's nothing much more to say; I dropped to the ground; I brushed off my clothes; I walked into the cottage; and there was my mother; and there was my brother; and this part goes out to the girl-friend: I loved love as much as any girl; I loved war as much as any guy; and I confess I considered swinging this body in and wrecking your fucking home; I confess I knew exactly how to do it; and it would have been spectacular; and I want you now to punish me; because I was being a girl and nothing but; because I was the only daughter of the man; because I kicked that guy's cart as hard as I could; and, fine, I meant to kick it that hard; and yes, there was trash all over the place; and yes, there was a sound like a sound you've never heard; and people were laughing; and the guy, the poor guy: you've never seen a sadder face; not even on my mother; not even on my brother; and it was going to snow; and then it was snowing; my God; I was totally wrecked; but yes, I had left him at the bar; yes, I got this body home; I knew how to do things so no one really got hurt; look, girlfriend; there were times things seemed all right; there were nights my father came home on time; and those nights, some, we ate at the table; and some of those nights, we stared at the same storm through the screen; and some of those nights when my mother was sleeping and my brother was sleeping, I stood with my father under the tree;

COWBOYS

There are some who say I did not kill my father.

Not technically they mean.

But the ones who say I did not kill my father are the ones who want to have sex with me.

They say I did not kill my father because they cannot have sex with a woman who killed.

What I mean is they cannot have sex with a woman who carries, though all women carry, an unbearable weight.

So they mix me another drink, they laugh, they say, You did not kill your father.

What they think they believe and what they truly believe: two different things.

I am still able to lie there nights, but I am unable to do much more than that.

Meaning I am still able to lie there nights, but I am unable to stick around in the mornings.

Meaning I am unable to lie there pretending I want what it is I'm supposed to want.

Because of this and because of that. And I cannot pretend to be anything other than the result of this and that.

When the doctor called at four a.m., waked me from a dream I can almost remember, something about chasing dogs in a field, something about a fence, he introduced himself as the doctor.

He said, I am doctor such-and-such, in this uptight voice, this deadpan voice. And I laughed and said, You're who. I said, Who is this.

My brother was also on the line. My brother was in Boston. The doctor was in Baltimore. And I was in a place called Warrensburg, Missouri. I was in Warrensburg, Missouri, for a job I was trying to quit. When I mention Warrensburg, Missouri, people say, Where the fuck is that.

I tell them there are cowboys there. I tell them there are tornadoes that can blow your house across the state. There are brown recluse spiders, I tell them, in every corner of every room. It's a shit hole, I tell them.

And there I was in it, trying my best to sleep right through it, a doctor telling me, at four a.m., please, to please be serious.

I was not always serious, and somehow the doctor already knew this, knew perhaps because I laughed when he said he was the doctor. Or perhaps he knew because my brother told him I would not be serious. Or perhaps he knew because when he told me to kill my father, I laughed again.

He did not, of course, use the word *kill.* He had another word, a series of words, a more technical way of wording.

The doctor sounded exhausted, and my brother sounded exhausted. My brother and his wife had a one-year-old boy. The boy was always crying in the background. My brother was always saying, Shh.

My brother always had circles under his eyes. They were bluish, the circles, and they made him look beaten down.

You look like Dad, I said to him once.

Fuck you, he said to me more than once.

We were no longer kids and this was a serious matter. The doctor had been up all night.

Trying to save your father, he said.

To no avail, he said, and I wondered at the word *avail,* wondered if the doctor got to be a doctor because of whatever it was he had that made him use that word.

I wanted something to eat. I wanted to run downstairs in the massive house I was renting in Warrensburg, Missouri, and root through the refrigerator for the leftovers. The leftovers were in take-out containers, and I wanted to bring them up to my bed, switch on the TV, settle into that blue-lit space.

The doctor said my father had flatlined several times. I knew the word *flatlined* from my ex, who had flatlined three times when we were together. He had flatlined, my ex, because he was an addict, and being an addict, as it turns out, will make you flatline. After the first time, my mother, a nurse, said, He'll never be the same. But he was the same, as it turned out, because he flatlined again. After the third time, we broke up. I'd like to say we broke up because I'd had enough, but really he broke up with me for another woman, a thinner woman, a paler woman, the veins too vivid through her face, and she eventually flatlined too, and she eventually died from this, but he did not.

He became a firefighter.

I moved to Warrensburg, Missouri.

The whole world just went on.

The doctor said my father would be a vegetable, and upon hearing this word, I imagined a plate. I imagined vegetables on this plate.

One does not want to imagine this. One wants to imagine one's father running through a field, arms spread, something dynamic like that.

Something totally made up like that.

My father would never have run through a field.

He was mad, yes, but he was not that kind of mad. He was the other kind. He was ferocious.

And besides, what field. In Baltimore, where we all were before we all weren't, there were no fields, just streets of nothing and more nothing, just my ex knocking on some boarded-up door, just me waiting in the car.

But here, where I was now, where I am no longer, in Warrensburg, Missouri, there were fields.

The doctor said my name.

He said, Please.

My brother said my name.

I had a decision to make. I had a serious decision to make, because I was the older kid. Though, as stated, I was not the more serious of the two. And my serious brother, with his serious boy screaming his head off in some dark room in their serious city, was waiting for me to do the right thing.

This was years ago, and I'm telling you this because the story came to me today for no real reason, just because I happened to see a guy digging through the trash, and I was like, You again. I was like, Get out of there.

And I'm telling you this, because some have been wondering why I am the way I am.

Which is to say a mess.

Which is to say a lot of things.

I could not at first kill my father. I at first said no. I said, Not as long as he's still breathing.

But he isn't breathing, said the doctor.

Not technically, he said.

The doctor sounded fed up. But not fed up with the limitations of science. And not with the limitations of the human body.

Meaning not fed up how I was.

A man I knew in Warrensburg, Missouri, a man I knew from the job I needed to quit, had been bitten by a brown recluse. He'd rolled over it one night in bed and got bitten in the ass. When he told me the story I laughed. I was like, Why were you naked. He was like, Wrong question. Because he was trying to tell me the bite dissolved the skin on his ass. Because he was trying to tell me that this just wasn't right.

The technical term is *necrotized*.

The point is I was not always serious.

No, the point is we're limited.

The doctor said, A machine is making him breathe.

He did not use the word *machine*.

I said I would have to call my mother to get her advice, and my brother said, Don't be a dumbass, and the doctor sighed in that way that the assholes I have dated since this night sigh when they don't get what they want.

Like the restaurant is out of chicken wings. Like the beer is flat. Like I'm trying to convince them I'm a terrible person. Like I'm already stepping into my skirt.

I'm already reaching for the doorknob, a bigger whore than they want me to be.

The sigh applies pressure to the woman. Then the woman is supposed to give them what they want.

Which is to say the woman is then supposed to perform.

Which is to say the woman is then supposed to know the subtle difference between being a woman and performing one.

I said, I'm calling our mother.

My brother said, Don't.

I thought I could get her on the line. I didn't know if it would work. It involved disconnecting the call. It involved dialing her number. It involved reconnecting the call, hoping everyone was still on the line.

The metaphor is unintentional.

I mean of disconnection.

There is no intentional metaphor in this story.

There is no intentional meaning in this story.

I would not subject you to intentional meaning.

I would not subject you to some grand scheme.

My mother was in Miami. Which wasn't where she should have been. But I wasn't where I should have been. No one was, when you think about it. I mean when you really think about it. I don't mean anything deep about anything deep. I just mean I was confused. Yet I disconnected, pressed some buttons, and there was my mother. Then I reconnected, and there we all were.

I said, They want me to kill Dad.

My mother had left my father thirty years before. There is no reason to go into the details. Suffice it to say it was his fault, as if that wasn't already clear.

I mean look at me. Look at my history.

I was not calling my mother because she loved my father. I was not even calling her because she was my mother. I was calling her because she was a nurse. I hoped that because she was a nurse she would tell me the right thing to do. I'm not talking morally. I'm talking medically. She knew about this. Though of course once she was wrong. Once she was dead wrong. I mean when my ex flatlined the first time. When she said, He'll never be the same. She was, of course, dead wrong. He was one hundred percent the same. He was one hundred percent the same in every way.

Impossible, a doctor might have said.

Not impossible, I might have said.

He was a vegetable going under, a vegetable coming back.

But his heart, a doctor might have said.

I might have laughed.

I might have said something regrettable.

My mother said, What.

My brother said, Tell her.

The doctor said, He flatlined.

My mother said, You have to kill him.

She did not, of course, use these words. I don't know why I'm being so melodramatic. She used technical terms. She said, Take him off the respirator. She said, It's the right thing to do. She said, Trust me. She said, I need to go, though. She said, I need to get to work. She said, I'm sorry.

And because I more often than not do the wrong thing, I said fine.

A few days later, because I was older, because the decision was mine, I would donate my father's body to science. I would do this over the phone, and the conversation would be recorded. A woman would ask me questions I had not before this heard.

Do you wish to donate the lungs.

Do you wish to donate the heart.

There were other organs one doesn't think of.

There were other things besides organs.

The tissue was to go to the tissue bank.

The eyes were to go to the eye bank.

There were other things I can't remember.

But it was the thought of the eyes removed from the head, the thought of the eyes going their own way, that made me cry.

I don't know why this was.

I was not suddenly a believer of the soul.

I was not suddenly a believer of anything.

It was just think about it.

And as I cried, the woman said, It's okay, said, Let it out, and I stopped crying and sat there, silent, and the recording went on, just recorded my breathing, the woman's breathing, the sound of static in the phone, and minutes passed.

And I thought for some reason of a night years before, me, my father, and my brother in some fast-food place. My brother was visiting home from college, and he was sticking his French fries into his milk shake, and I said, Sick, and he said, Fuck you, and I said, Fuck you, and he said, Try it, dumbass, and I stuck a French fry into the milk shake, and it was amazing. My father was poor then, always poorer the next day, living in some shit hole, like a hostel, like a hospital, like a halfway house, and my brother said he would take him to dinner. Anywhere you want, he said. My father wanted to go to the fast-food place. He met us there. He was filthy. His shirt was missing buttons. He ordered two cheeseburgers. He ordered onion rings. He ordered an orange soda. He ate too fast. And, watching us stick French fries into the milk shake, he said, You're both sick. But then he tried it too, and then he laughed, and then we ordered more French fries and another milk shake, and what I'm trying to say is, you should try it. What I'm trying to say is. What I'm trying to say is.

I did not donate the eyes to the eye bank. At some point I said, I can't.

The parts that didn't go to science were burned. And, no, I did not want the ashes. I told the woman to send the ashes to my brother. Because my brother was a better person than I was. He was a total asshole, I told the woman, but he was still a better person than I was. I said, He's a total asshole. But in the grand scheme, I said. In the big grand scheme, I said. And I laughed, meaning I really laughed, and the recording went on, and the woman cleared her throat, and I just kept on going.

The day the ashes arrived, my brother called me and said, What the fuck, and I said, What, and he said, What the fuck, and I said, Grow up.

There are no more details to tell.

There is no reason to go into the why of my father.

Or the why of madness, which I cannot answer.

Or the why of addiction, which I also cannot answer.

Or the why of poor, which I also cannot answer.

Suffice it to say it's always about a loss of something. Then a loss of some things. Then a loss of all things.

Then he was already dead, some might say.

What do you mean, I might say back.

If he had already lost everything, some might say, then he was already dead.

Yes, I might say.

Then you didn't kill him, some might say as they moved toward me.

That's not the point.

Then what is.

The doctor said he was sorry for our loss.

My brother said, You did the right thing.

Then a lot of serious shit happened in a lot of serious places. My mother drove to work. The doctor flipped a switch. My brother made coffee. The sun rose somewhere, set somewhere else. A brown recluse hunched in the dust.

And the truth is I don't always leave in the mornings.

Some mornings the guy wants to get to work, and so I have to leave, but the truth is I don't want to.

Some mornings I'm still lying in their beds, and they're like, You need to leave, and I just lie there staring at their backs.

Some mornings I note the rib cage. I note the organs seething beneath the rib cage. I note the fragility of what does not, at night, seem fragile.

Some mornings I am not the whore they want me to be.

I am not the killer they want me to be.

Some mornings I try to no avail. To absolutely no avail. To no avail I try, and they get up to make coffee, and I get up and step into my skirt, and I pull on my shirt and walk home.

And the woman performs happy woman on a sunny street.

The woman performs this all feels good this all feels really good.

The woman pulls it together. She pulls it tight. She further tightens that which tightens.

There were late nights he would call from a pay phone, a friend's house, a hospital, and because it was late, and because I was not poor, and because I was not ferociously mad, but, rather, mad mad, a machine answered my phone and lied that I wasn't there eating in bed, watching TV, lied that I would return the call.

The machine would then say, Hello, stranger.

The machine would then say, It's your father, stranger.

There were voices in the background.

There was traffic in the background.

I'm okay, stranger, the machine would then say.

There was screaming in the background.

There was me in my bedroom.

Pick up the phone, the machine would say loudly.

I know you're there, the machine would say louder.

There was me turning the TV all the way up.

There was every poor soul looking downward.

There was me not believing in the soul.

There was me waiting, counting seconds, staring at the wall.

My mother said good-bye and disconnected first. Then the doctor said good-bye and disconnected. After the doctor disconnected, there was silence, but I said, Hello. I was hoping my brother was still on the line. I wanted to laugh or something. I said hello again, but my brother had disconnected too.

And before I ran downstairs to the massive kitchen that was my kitchen, I sat on the edge of my bed, still holding the phone.

I imagined the doctor arriving home that morning.

I imagined the doctor taking off his scrubs, washing his hands, and climbing into bed with his beautiful wife.

I imagined him easing into his wife's heat, the way I once eased into my ex's heat.

Before we had a sense of what came next.

Before we had a sense that something came next.

Firefighting.

Warrensburg, Missouri.

Me in my bed eating cold lo mein.

Me eating egg rolls, watching TV.

You have to trust me.

There was no grand scheme.

I would quit my job. I would leave that place. I would cross the state line. I would cross another. I would cross another.

And here I am now in a different state.

There is the man digging through the trash.

There is the gem buried in the mess.

Listen. It was not a shit hole.

It was not that.

Call it what you will, but there were cowboys there, for God's sake, standing on corners in the biggest hats you have ever seen.

There were tornadoes that would send you into space.

There were spiders that would necrotize your ass.

There was a sky turning light. The same sky as everywhere turning light.

Call it what you will, but there I was, same as you were, under that sky.

There I was, just some poor soul. Same as you.

SUPERNOVA

When the plane crashed, I was all messed up. I was all kinds of all messed up. Because first we'd had drinks. Next we'd smoked. There were pills we'd taken from a bowl on the floor. The pills all did their different things. We liked not knowing what they would do. It didn't matter which way we went.

When the plane crashed, I was on a couch. I was in this place, Club Midnight. It was where we went when it got too late. Or there was nowhere else to go. A guy was sitting next to me. He was a guy I knew from school. He was a guy I hardly knew. It didn't matter that he was there. It was always a lot of us sitting there drinking. A lot of us always were sitting around.

There's nothing to say about the guy. This is not the place for adjectives. I wasn't even looking at him. The pills from the bowl had spilled to the floor. And no one was rushing to pick them up. I made no move to pick them up. I just sat there thinking they'd get crushed. I was waiting for the boot that would come to crush them. I was thinking of the sound the boot would make. I was thinking of the person attached to the boot. The beautiful person we all could blame.

At first the guy wasn't looking at me. But when the plane was falling from the sky, I felt him writing on my arm. And before he could finish what he was writing, I said, Stop.

I don't know how to tell the next part. It was like I knew a plane had crashed. Even though I was all messed up. Even though I was thousands of miles from the plane. It was like I had a premonition. Or I felt a reverberation. I mean I felt a crash push through my skin. Not from his pen. Not what you think. It was more like air pushing through. Or a song pushing through. It was more just like a ghost.

Winter was creeping in again. The holidays, again. I would not be doing much that year. The same thing I did every year. Going to my father's house. Not eating what my father made. Staring at my father across the table staring at me. Glaring across the table because he never let me do a thing. My father, who thought he'd saved my life.

The other kids all studied abroad. They came back home all better than me. They knew things I didn't know. There were lamp-lit roads they talked about. There were churches made of stone. There were whores in windows lit by red lights. I could see myself walking the lamp-lit roads. I could see myself small in a hollow church. I would be too far for my father to find. But my father said no to study abroad. You're not ready, he said. You don't study, he said.

It wasn't technically a crash. It was technically an explosion. It was technically a fireball. Technically, it was a lot of things. What I mean is, it was meant.

It then took just the sound of a plane. Or a trail of smoke. Or a shadow moving fast and wide across grass. And the terrible way my brain worked. The way my brain said duck. And fast. And now. And I would lie in the snow. I would lie under trees. I would wait for the plane to pass overhead. Or for the smoke to disappear. Or for my brain to tell me, Get up. Or for the plane to crash.

I knew the chance of a crash was small. A plane would not likely drop from the sky. I would not likely be crushed on the ground. It was all of it unlikely. And I knew that it wasn't just planes. That cars could swerve. That trains could derail. I'd once seen a bus that had gone off the road. It was upside down in a field. But this didn't make me afraid of buses. Because there was something different about crashing on land. I mean it was different from crashing to land.

As a kid I wanted to walk a tightrope. I'd seen a circus on TV. I'd watched it with my father. I liked the tightrope walker most. I liked the thin stick he held on to. And how he stared ahead to the other side. And how he would make it clear to that other side. Or how, perhaps, he would not.

There were photos all over of the crash. It's not enough to say raining metal. It's not enough to say twisted metal. Or that the people on the ground were stuck in the storm. Or that I wasn't there, of course, in the storm. Because I was thousands of miles away, of course. I was sitting around Club Midnight. And pills were spilled out onto the floor. And a guy was writing on my arm. He wrote the first four letters of my name. I imagine he planned to write the fifth. But I said, Stop.

There was a service in a church. I went because it was right to go. I went because everyone went. Before the service, we stood outside. Someone had something to smoke. Someone else had pills. We went to the service all messed up. I was too messed up to feel a thing. It wasn't a big deal, being messed up. The whole world was a mess.

Then were the times lying flat in the snow. It didn't make sense, my lying flat. I know this now. It would not have saved me, lying flat, from a storm of metal crashing.

To my friends I said, I'm fine. I said, I am. But they looked at me like, You're not fine. But I am, I said. Because I was, I thought. Because I didn't know her well enough to be anything other than fine.

The guy was laughing at me. I was too messed up to laugh. My tongue felt covered in fur. Clouds had formed, and I fell into them, one by one. I said, My tongue. I said, My God. I didn't mean to say this. I didn't mean to say anything. I didn't want a conversation. It had started to snow, and I wanted to go outside. Because the snow just seemed like more than snow. It was something about the light. I didn't know what it was. But the guy said, Your tongue, and laughed again. And then I was falling into him. And if I must use an adjective, right now, right here, I would use *beautiful.*

I know I shouldn't have been driving. The roads were a mess. Murder, my father would have said. Murder, every time it snowed. But there I was, rising from the couch. There I was, surrounded by clouds. Next I was in the driver's seat. And there he was beside me. And there were the holiday lights in windows. And the lit-up trees in windows. And the reflection of my car. And the reflection of us inside the car. And there was my building. There were the stairs leading to my door.

I said I wanted to walk a tightrope. My father said, Do you want to be killed. I didn't want to be killed. I wanted to be something else. I wanted to be between living and not living. Just for the time it would take to walk the tightrope. Just for the time it would take to make it to the other side. Or for the time it would take to fall. Over my dead body, my father said. I would go to school like everyone else. I would read and write like everyone else. I would graduate like everyone else. I would go to college. I would get a job. I would live in a house. I would have kids. And eventually I, like everyone else, would die.

There's nothing to say about the service. Someone spoke. Then someone else spoke. Then someone played guitar. Because she played guitar. Because it's how she would have wanted it. That's what everyone said. She would have wanted it that way. As if anyone ever could really know. I hardly even knew the girl. She went to my school. I sometimes smoked with her after class. I sometimes saw her in Club Midnight. But it was always a lot of us drinking. It was her and it was the guy from the couch. It was others too, and we sometimes talked. And perhaps I lit her cigarette once. Perhaps she cupped her hands around mine. But she went off to study abroad. And I, as you know, did not.

In my bed we talked about who knows what. Those nouns that emerge in bed. What passes for deep. Life. God. I know you know how I must have felt. And at some point we just fell asleep. And while we were sleeping, saviors were being called upon. Saviors were showing up to help. Bodies were pulled from the wreckage. The scene was played and replayed and replayed. And we lay there.

But this story is not about the guy. He just happens to be in it. Like paint on the walls. Like sound in the air. Like hydrogen. Like oxygen.

It's a miracle, my father said. I saved your life, he said. My father had food on his face. The TV droned in another room. The wine was almost gone. A holiday at my father's house. A miracle, he said.

When the phone rang, my dreams were of ringing. And when I waked and answered, I meant not to answer. But there I was, saying hello. And there was someone else saying, Wait. Saying, Get up, get up. I already knew it was something big. I'd already had a premonition. If I were someone else, I would tell you more. I would tell you what I was told. But I'll just say the world was then an open door letting cold air in.

And I'll say it was like a supernova, how I thought of supernovas. A split second of silence. An explosion in the sky. Then a shooting outward and shooting outward. And some things landed. And some things burned. And some flew through clouds. Or fell through clouds. Or crashed into bodies they never knew until they crashed.

I'm sure the people in the bus all died. There was no way, the bus turned over like that, they did not. I wanted to drive out onto the field to see if I could help. But I kept on driving up the road. I had somewhere to be that night. There was no way I could have helped.

I kicked the guy awake. I said, You should leave. I said, Please leave. I said, Leave. And I left too. I watched the guy walk through the snow. I found my car parked terribly. I didn't notice the tires at first. I didn't see that two of the tires were slashed. It looked almost right, the car tilted like that. And I drove it like that. And I kept on driving, until I found help.

After the service, we stood outside. The guy broke down in a way that made me ashamed. He tried to hold my hand. I told him, please, to not do that. I told him, please, to go away. I wanted to be alone, I told him. I didn't want to be touched, I told him. I walked to behind the church. I know I should have been nicer to him. But the holidays were over. There was too much snow on the ground. And I had a thought. I thought, You don't know when your last snowfall is. It was such a fucking stupid thought.

But this was the shift, if you're looking for one. I was leaning against the back of the church. I was saying words that sounded like prayer. I was saying words that sounded like *fuck* and *help*.

And I heard a plane. And my brain said duck. My brain said now and now and now. There was a lot going on. There was snow, and there was the sound of snow. The moon was out when it shouldn't have been. The moon seemed close enough to touch. And there was the guy in the way of the moon. He said to get up. But I couldn't get up. And he said, Get up.

A mechanic looked at my tires. Someone doesn't like you, he said. But it was a miracle, he said, that I'd made it there. I agreed it was a miracle. It was a miracle, driving on two slashed tires. A miracle had pushed me hard through the snow. The mechanic told me to wait in a room. There was tinsel on the floor. There was a fake tree in the corner. There was the smell of oil and the smell of smoke. And the snow was really coming down. And the mechanic was beautiful, with black beneath every nail.

I could clearly see the scene on the ground. And if I had been someone else, I might have been putting out fires. I might have been pulling bodies out from the wreckage. I might have felt heroic, diving headfirst into the mess. And if I had been some-one else, I might have been a body in the mess. I might have been a body pulled from the wreckage. Instead of a body on a couch. Then in a car. Then on a bed. Instead of a body starting something it would have to stop.

I could clearly see the scene on the ground. But I couldn't see the scene inside the plane.

At dinner, I asked my father why things were the way they were. And my father said, Not my fault. Because it wasn't my father's fault, the world. He was too small to take the blame. He was only a person, for God's sake. It was no one person's fault, the world. Nothing that small was ever to blame for something that big. I said, Then whose fault is it. And he said, Not mine.

I often imagined crossing the tightrope. I knew to stare straight to the other side. I knew to hold the stick steady. I knew to force the crowd to be silent. And then, when I reached the other side, I knew to force it to explode.

The mechanic would keep my car overnight. I'd shredded the tires. Shredded the rims. Something was ruined underneath. He drove me home in a tow truck. I tried to think of things to say. Like something about how he chose his job. Like what, was he good at fixing things. Or did he just like cars. But it was such a terrible-feeling day. I wanted to tell the mechanic that. But I hardly knew the mechanic. And I hardly knew the girl.

If I were someone else, I would make something up. I would say she and I did things together. Or we were best friends. Or we were in love. But I'll just say I lit her cigarette once. I'll say I was shaking as I lit it. I'll say the fire kept going out. I'll say it turned into a private joke. I'll say, Enough.

I looked as the pen scratched down my arm. It had felt like a feather. Or like an ant. But I was thinking ghost. And I said, Stop. I meant, Go. I meant, Stay. I meant, God. And I stood. And he stood. And on our way out the door we crushed the pills with our boots.

I could clearly see the scene from the ground. It looked, from the ground, like meteors falling. Not like plane parts falling.

But like fire falling. I could see the town go up in flames. And I would hear its name every day for the rest of my life.

The mechanic said to have a good day. But it was already not a good day. It was already a terrible day. And I thought to invite him in. I would take his coat. I would make him tea. I would tell him about my night. That it was very good and it was very bad. That it could have been love. That it would never be love. And I would dig out the black from beneath every one of his nails.

But I sat in the tow truck for a moment longer than I should have. A song was playing on the radio. I knew the song from some other time. There were holiday lights in all of the windows. There were holiday lights in all of the trees. It was warm in the truck. And outside it would not be.

The night before, I'd slept the deepest sleep. And I waked not knowing what I was waking into. And the phone kept on ringing. Someone saying, Get up, get up. My father saying, I saved your life. My father saying, Miracle. The guy in my bed saying something.

The night before, he'd told me a story. He was half-asleep. He whispered it into my hair. It was about a time at Club Midnight. A time he was messed up and had to leave. It was snowing. It was morning. He was waiting alone for the bus. But then this woman came walking through the snow. The woman wasn't wearing a coat. She was holding a knife. She held the knife up to his face. She said, Give me your money. But the guy had no money. And the woman said, Do you want to be killed. Then he started to fall asleep on me. And I said, How did you answer. But he'd already fallen asleep.

When I imagined falling from the tightrope, I imagined what I would pass on my way to the ground. The hats of the people in the crowd. The necks of the people in the crowd. Their shoes as I crashed as hard as I could. I imagined breaking every bone. I would lie there waiting for someone to help. And a guy would rush to save me. And the crowd would be thinking terrible thoughts. Because I fell. Because I was saved.

I picked up my car the following day. But the mechanic wasn't there. It was another mechanic I didn't like. He gave me my keys and walked away. I knew I was going to cry. And I didn't know why I was going to cry. And I didn't want to cry right there. So I went into the restroom. It was an awful room. It was the smallest room. And I didn't want to cry in there either. So I ran water in the sink. I scrubbed my hands as hard as I could. I scrubbed my face and neck and arms. I scrubbed extra hard at the first four letters of my name. And how unsettling to see its faint bluish trace. How unsettling never to see it again.

I don't know who slashed my tires. I sometimes think it was her. Because it happened when she was flying. I mean it happened when she was dying. She was becoming a ghost in a world of ghosts and almost-ghosts.

I sometimes think she meant it as a joke. Because she and I had a private joke once. But I mostly think it was a desperate stranger on the road.

But of course I knew her. I lied to you. Of course I lied.

This story is not about me. As it turns out, I'm just a detail. Like the sky. Like the snow. Like the car you think was real. Or the bus you think was real. Or the plane you think was real. Or the premonition that, you should know, was not.

It wasn't technically a crash. It was technically an explosion. It was technically a lot of things. Like the end of things. Not of everything. Not to everyone.

And I would hear its name each day for the rest of my life. Every day from that point on. Fucking stupid as that is.

I stared across the table at my father. I asked again whose fault it was. My father tried not to look at me. He said, Not mine. And I said, I know. I said, But whose. And he said, Not mine. He said, Not mine. He lifted up his empty glass. He threw the glass at the wall. The glass shattered. Dinner was over. The holiday, over. It was snowing again. The roads were a mess. I put on my coat. I walked to the door. Over my dead body, my father said. Murder, he said. The roads were a wreck. But I had new tires.

And I had somewhere to be that night. We would all meet up at Club Midnight. I would sit on a couch. I would drink my drinks. There would be pills to take, and clouds would form.

For a while, I would hear a plane and fall to the snow. And I would wait for the plane to pass overhead. Or for the plane to crash. Or for my brain to tell me what next.

And once, lying in the snow, I watched as a bird crashed into a bird. I hadn't known such a thing could happen. And there was no one around to tell it to. And I don't know what I would have said, besides.

And once, lying in the snow, I watched as the moon moved across the sky. And I hadn't known that one could watch it move.

And once I looked up into a face. And if I were someone else, I would tell you more. But this is not the place for adjectives. This is not the place for any words. Not even, Get up. Not even, You're fine. Not even, It's not your fault.

SIGNIFIER

Because words are about desire and desire is about the long-tailed birds in the trees.

And desire is about the long-tailed birds as long-tailed birds. Not as metaphor. Not as signifier. Not as anything other than what they are but long-tailed birds switching from branch to branch.

Predatory, this guy I once met called these long-tailed birds.

Magpies, he called them, because they were, and what did I know of birds.

They will chew off your face, he said.

He said, Your pretty face, and touched my face.

When I watch through a window, I feel watched through the window. When I press my face to a screen, I feel pressed from the other side.

But nothing in trees wants to know what goes on in rooms. Even when I scratch like a cat at the screen. Even when I make sounds with my tongue and teeth.

And when I send words from my brain to the tops of the trees, by which I mean stars, by which I mean something else, the universe, even then.

I was taught to do this as a child. I was taught this would work, sending words from my brain. Taught by whom, I can't remember.

It was someone who knew about that which listens.

It was someone lying still on the grass, saying, Come here pretty, saying, Not you.

It was someone who knew the universe.

It was a father, of course I remember.

Some father lying still on the grass.

Some father still lying after dark.

As the world went on around him.

And the world went on without him.

But this isn't a story about the father.

It's a story about a hike in the woods. It was me and this guy and this friend he had. I never wanted to go on the hike. I mean I never thought it would be a real hike. I thought we'd find a rock, just me and the guy, and sit and stare at the view.

But the friend was in from out of town. He wanted to go on the hike with us. He knew all the trails that no one else knew.

And he would drive, the guy said.

Come on, he said.

We were standing at my door. I hadn't dressed for walking up trails. I'd only dressed for sitting on a rock. I'd dressed for charming this one guy. And here was the guy, dressed to go on an actual hike. And there was the friend, dressed for a hike, as well.

The friend called out, Do you have a hat.

He called out, Do you have real shoes.

His voice was such a tough guy's voice. It seemed like work to talk like that. All the work it took to try to be that guy.

I said, No.

I said, Do you.

He was wearing sturdy shoes. And a sturdy coat. And he stood all tough. It seemed like too much work.

He said, I have real shoes.

I laughed.

I said, Do you.

Trust me when I say I wasn't flirting. I didn't like the friend. Though later, this will all sound like a lie. Later, you will think new things of me. You will think some things you don't think now.

But trust me it was the guy I liked. I wanted a date just me and him. We'd sit on a rock and pretend some things about the universe. About beauty. About other abstractions I didn't understand.

I said to no one, Give me a cigarette.

I didn't smoke. But I sometimes wanted a cigarette. Smoking made me feel better at times. I can't explain it. But of course the friend walked up to me. And of course he struck the match.

And at what point does one tire of performance. At what point is it all just tiring. The friend's performance of guy. My performance of girl. The guy I liked not even stepping in. Not lighting my cigarette himself. Too scared to get that close to me.

Just standing there like some dumb fuck.

The friend just stood there, dumb, as well.

To say I had them where I wanted them.

They were dumbstruck more than dumb.

Because I was just so fucking charming.

Because I was always just so fucking this.

Just ask my father.

Just ask his ladies.

They would say, What a charming little thing.

They would say, What a pretty little thing.

I could eat you up, is what they would say.

Inside the woods was darker than out. There were birds and bird sounds all around. The friend knew all about birds. He told us what he knew about birds. He told us what he knew about trees. I pretended not to listen. What did I care what tree was what. What birds.

Though I liked to look upward through the leaves. I wouldn't have told this to anyone. That it gave me a feeling I can't explain.

And at times I considered stepping off the trail. Of running wild through the woods. It would have been something, I thought. To get lost in the trees. To imagine there was no other world.

And I would have stepped off the trail if the friend hadn't called out, Come on.

There was something he wanted to show us. It was up ahead. He was walking way too fast.

He called back to me, Let's go.

Then he was running, and the guy was running, and I didn't want to run. I wasn't dressed to run. And I didn't know what was up ahead. So I walked at my own slow pace.

There were stories from childhood I'd read of the woods. There were pictures in books I'd stared at at night. In the pictures the trees had eyes and teeth.

And there were other stories I knew of the woods. There were things that happened in the woods at night. There were woods by our house and I was told stay away.

I was told stay away from other things too. Like the dog next door, yet I fed him bones through the fence. Like the two dumb guys who came around. They wanted to fuck me. They were both so dumb.

Like my father.

I told myself, Stay away.

He will destroy you, is what I told myself.

Run away, is what I told myself.

He will turn you into him, I told myself.

You are not that whore, I told myself.

But look at me hiking in completely wrong shoes. Look at me in completely wrong clothes. Look at my fucking hair.

From far ahead the friend said, Come on, and the guy said, Come on, but I walked slowly, staring up into leaves.

My father would say, Don't go in the woods.

I would mock him, Don't go into the woods.

Then I would go.

At first I didn't know what to expect.

Darkness, perhaps.

The terrible sound of owls.

Or worse.

The terrible acts of guys.

My body surrounded by what surrounded.

My body eaten, the rest left for worms.

But it wasn't any of that.

It was far worse, of course, than that.

The friend said, Come on.

The guy said, Let's go.

Their voices sounded far away. And here was my chance to step off the trail. My chance to save what was left to save.

But there I was, running to catch up with them. There I was, some scared-as-shit girl. I was some scared-as-shit child. Running in wrong shoes up the trail. Scared to be left alone.

And there were the guys, waiting for me.

Then the woods opened up and we were in a place. It was

like childhood. Not mine, of course, but the childhood I wished I'd had.

There was what one could call a clearing, and there were trees. There was what one could call a waterfall.

And there was me looking at the waterfall. There was the friend looking at it too. There was the guy sticking his hands into the water.

I didn't want anything in that moment. I mean I didn't want to want anything. I don't know exactly what I mean.

I know I wanted to be a different person than I was.

I wanted to see the waterfall as beautiful.

I wanted to be less beautiful than the waterfall.

I wanted to want to be that.

But when my arms began to ache, for we'd been all day hiking, I said, My arms.

The guy said, Your arms.

The friend said, What do you mean your arms.

He walked over to me.

He said, It should be your legs.

He said, Where.

I held out my arms. He touched them. And the guy just watched. He did nothing to stop it. He too was too scared.

After the hike, we drank in the car. And after we drank, we went for a ride. It was early evening and summer and perfect. And I loved in that moment the sound of the crickets. I loved in that moment the color of the sky. And the back of both guys' heads in the front.

As a child, I could never make up my mind. I would want both toys. I would want both dolls.

Old maid, my father always said.

You'll end up with nothing, he always said.

Or both, I always said.

If one was truly charming, one could have both.

Just look at me charming my father's ladies as a child.

Look at them giving me things to keep.

I would hold out my hands, which were filled and refilled.

And look at me getting the toy and the game.

Getting both new dolls.

Getting both dumb guys.

Look at me hiking up my skirt.

Look at them now all scared of me.

Look at me running through woods.

I was utterly disgraceful.

Just look at the sun about to set.

Just look.

The guy had to piss. The friend pulled off to the side. The guy went into the woods. The friend and I stood by the car. At first it was nothing, just standing. But then he lifted me onto the hood of the car. It was just to be funny, I was thinking. But I wasn't thinking. I mean to say there was no thought.

But that's not true. Because I was thinking something as he lifted me up.

I was thinking of something wrong to think.

And when his face was near mine, I thought of the guy.

And when he said, Pretty face, I thought, Pretty face.

And when I said to stop, he said, Stop what.

And when it was me on the hood of the car, it wasn't me on the hood of the car.

And when I was a girl on the hood of the car, I was a guy on the hood of the car.

I didn't know where to put my hands.

The guy had come out from the woods by then. He was

standing at the woods' edge. He was looking at us like I don't know what.

Like, Fuck you two. Like, I will kill you two.

I want to say I was drunk. But I was more that thing after drunk. That thing between drunk and sleep. Or drunk and regret. Or drunk and drunk again.

And the truth is I knew where to put my hands.

Because I was predatory.

That's not the word.

I was perverted.

That's not it.

I was something though.

Just some little thing.

Just some charming little thing.

I wish I could give you a climactic moment. But there is no climactic moment in this. There is no such thing here as climactic. In a story about a hike, there is only a circling around and around.

In a story about me and guys, there is only a circling around.

And in a story about a story.

In a story about the father.

Mine taught me all the wrong things.

Mine taught me how to be that girl.

Mine taught me how to be that guy.

So thank you, Father, thank you, thank you.

And thank you, trees, for not noticing me.

Thank you, birds, for not noticing me.

Thank you, windows, for keeping the universe on its side.

For keeping me on mine.

My father would wake me mornings, his face too close, shout, Rise and shine, in my face, and I wanted his face far away.

And I wanted it farther and farther.

And when it was as far away as it could be, it still wasn't far enough.

It was still right there, my father's face, in front of my face.

My father ready to give me away.

My father ready to throw me away.

Whenever you're ready, he always said.

I'm waiting, he said.

Old maid, he said.

Still waiting, he said.

Then he died.

I should say there were moments in childhood worth something. I made tents from sheets like anyone. I dug holes in the yard.

My father threw me into the air, caught me.

He threw me into the air, caught me.

He threw me into the air.

It wasn't so different in moments. I wasn't so different from you.

I was falling, like you, for something.

The guy stood by the edge of the woods. I wanted him to stop looking at us. I wanted him to stop looking like that. And I would have said something smart, like, Take a picture. But I was thinking instead that he could get hurt. I don't know why. Perhaps it was the shadows on the road. Or his smallness next to trees. I was thinking of the stories of the woods at night. I knew what could happen in the woods. There were monsters. There were witches. There were killers.

So I sent a thought to the universe. And I sent it again. I sent it again.

And when he moved from the woods, I was a believer in something.

And when he reached the car, I was not.

Because then I remembered.

What.

I just remembered.

What.

Desire is desire for recognition, and I was controlled by desire just like you.

I was fucked up just like you.

The guy walked up to the car, said, What's going on, and I said, What.

And he looked at the friend and said, You know what, and the friend laughed and said, What.

Now, I see why this was wrong. All of it. I see.

But in that moment I was too in love.

I don't mean with the friend. I don't mean with the guy.

The ride home was the radio loud. It was none of us saying a word. It was my drinking what was left to drink. It was the friend dropping the guy off first. It was the guy slamming the door.

Then it was just me and the friend in the car. And we pulled up to my place. He followed me inside.

I swear I was thinking, No, and, No.

I swear.

This is not the time to ask me what I was. Though if you did, I might say a child. I might say the child I was as a child, landing hard on the grass and lying there until the world went dark.

It was my father who said to send your thoughts.

It was he who said to tell the universe what you want.

Back then I wanted the things one wants: a doll, a dog.

Back then I pictured the universe as a thing one could understand: a two-dimensional scene with grass at the bottom, stars at the top.

My father would say, Don't tell me, as he stumbled across the yard toward some lady waiting on the grass.

He would say, Tell the universe what you want, as they stumbled to the car.

Night would scatter across the grass, across the house.

I would meet the guys at the edge of the woods.

I would be that monster in the woods. That killer. That witch. That girl running wild, her skirt hiked to her waist.

At some point you become something other than girl. At some point you become confused. Then you're that from that point on.

I waked the next day and he'd left. I suppose he just got in his car, went home.

It's not like we had some kind of thing.

It's not like he was a permanent thing.

It's not like anything was.

The dog next door. My father's ladies. My dolls.

I don't know where these things went.

And I don't know where my father went.

I mean he died, of course.

I mean nobody knows where he went, of course.

To the other side.

Dumb thought.

I don't know what to make of that.

How it wants to be deep.

How it isn't deep.

And I don't know what to make of you.

How you're just like me.
How you think you aren't.
And I don't know what to make of birds.
How they stab their faces at the cold, hard ground.
How they're fucked up just like us.

UNDERTHINGS

My boyfriend hit me in the face with a book. It was an accident, his hitting me. He only meant to hand me the book. He meant to hand the book back to me. But my face was in its path, he said. It was in its way, he said. And so the book connected with my face. And so here we are.

I guess I must have closed my eyes. Because I didn't see the book hit my face. But I heard it hit, if you can imagine. It made a sound against my face. I can't describe the sound it made. But imagine, if you can, the sound.

Then I watched at the mirror as a red mark spread across my face. It transformed my face into another face. By which I mean a face I knew. By which I mean a lot of things.

It was an accident, his hitting me in the face with the book. Accident, he said, dropping the book, holding up his hands. Accident, I later said to my brother. Bullshit, my brother said. He hit you with a fucking book, he said.

As kids, my brother did his thing, I did mine. His things were, for the most part, boy things. Mine were, for the most part, not. But they were not what I would call girl things. I was not a girl who did girl things. I was a girl who worked on puzzles. These were puzzles that took weeks to solve. And when I solved a puzzle, and I always solved them, I felt brilliant.

After my boyfriend went back to sleep, I walked outside. Outside was the rest of the world. Outside were the people of the world. It was a regular day for people. There was work and there were the other things that people do. And there I was with them, walking with them, through rain.

My father wanted to become an astronaut. But he did not become an astronaut. Because, he said, he would not have passed the physical. So my father went into business. He became a businessman. There were sales and deals and men like my father. There was a product of some sort he sold. It was nothing like being an astronaut. But there was hope for my brother, my father said. He could still become one, he said.

My boyfriend was brutally killed in his dreams. Sometimes he was stabbed. Sometimes someone's hands were squeezing tightly around his throat. And there were zombies too. And witches too. And sharp-toothed animals chasing him through woods. It was called night terrors, what he had, and he would wake up screaming and run through the room. On the worst of these nights, my boyfriend and I were terrified. We never knew what was going on. We would often stay up all night, those nights, waiting for the room to turn light. But they were often funny, those nights, the next day.

We had all been out the night before. It was me, my boyfriend, my brother, and a girl. It was an upscale bar my boyfriend liked. My brother did not like upscale things. He liked the trashy bars in his part of the city. He liked the trashy girls in those trashy bars. My brother thought my boyfriend was a prick. And my boyfriend thought my brother was a prick. But I should say it was my birthday. That we were at the upscale bar to celebrate my birthday. My boyfriend bought the first round of drinks. And my brother bought another round. And my boyfriend bought another. And at some point my brother pushed up his sleeve. He wanted to arm-wrestle my boyfriend. He said he would wrestle him through the fucking table. My brother was big. He worked at a gym. It was a gym where big guys went to get bigger. My boyfriend was not so big. But he was tougher than my brother. He was tough in another way. The bar was crowded and people were staring. My brother stuck his elbow to the table. Then my boyfriend stuck his elbow to the table. Then my brother and my boyfriend gripped each other's hands.

I walked all the way to my brother's part of the city. At my brother's place, I rang the bell, then rang again. Then I called his name from the street. I was surprised to hear the front door's click. Surprised to see my brother standing in his doorway. And before I was even down the hallway, he was looking too hard at my face. It was terrible, how he was looking. Terrible, how banged up I was. I had seen those banged-up women before. I had seen them on streets, all terrible looking, all banged up. It was wrong, the way my brother was looking. Dumb, how we were just standing there. I said, Is your girl here still. He said, She's not my girl. But is she here, I said. Fuck you, he said. I knew my brother way too well. I knew he fucked her and sent

63

her home. He often fucked them and showed them the door. I held up my hand for a high five. My brother was that guy, always holding up his. I said, High five. But he left me hanging, my hand up high.

There was a day I had solved a difficult puzzle. And I went into my brother's bedroom and told my brother how I had solved it. And my brother said he understood how I had solved the puzzle. And he suggested a different way of solving it. And his way of solving it was somehow better than mine. And it was in this moment I saw his brilliance. I hadn't seen this brilliance before. And I knew it was more brilliant than mine.

I should say again we were in the bar to celebrate this thing that went right, once, years before, the thing being, simply, my being there, that miraculous spark that kept on going, and there I was.

And I should say that my brother won, of course. He slammed my boyfriend's knuckles into the table as hard as he could. People in the bar applauded. The girl kissed my brother on his mouth. My brother went to buy a round of drinks. My boyfriend was angry and he looked very angry. Your brother's the biggest prick, he said. But my brother was not the biggest prick. He was buying us a round of drinks. He's not the biggest prick, I said. There are way bigger pricks, I said. And my boyfriend said, What does that mean. And I guess this was when the fight began. My boyfriend said, It must mean something. You must mean me, he said.

It was dumb how we were just standing there. I said, Let me in, but my brother didn't move. I said, Let me fucking in, but he just stood there staring at my face. So I pushed past my brother and went to the kitchen. His kitchen was the worst kitchen ever. It could barely fit two people at once. It could barely fit even one. The kitchen table was not in the kitchen. It was outside the kitchen. It was against a wall in the other room. In the refrigerator was a case of beer. I took a beer. My brother squeezed into the kitchen. He grabbed my arm. He shook the beer from my hand. It rolled to somewhere, to under something. Then my brother pulled me from the refrigerator. He pulled me from the kitchen. He pushed me into a chair. Then he sat in a chair. And we sat, like anyone, on any morning, at the kitchen table.

My mother left three dolls in the house and my father gave them to me. They were my mother's dolls from when she was a kid. But I was not a girl who played with dolls. And I did not want my mother's things, besides. So I gave the dolls to my brother. They wore dresses from other countries. My brother named them girls' names. He kept them in a row on his dresser. I don't think he ever played with the dolls. I think he just wanted to keep them like that, in a row.

My boyfriend walked ahead of me home from the bar. I was fine with not walking next to him. We were in a fight, and I was fine. I was used to our fights. I was used to the door slamming in my face. I almost loved when the door slammed in my face. Because it meant my boyfriend would sleep on the couch.

On my brother's kitchen table were dried dots of something red. There were crumbs of something white. It was a mess, the table, a mess, the whole room. My brother reached toward me as if to grab me. What happened to your face, he said. And he could have grabbed my shirt or my arm, but he didn't. What happened to your face, I said. I was pushing the crumbs into the dots. My brother was watching me do this. Tell me, he said. You tell me, I said. He was watching me pick off each red dot, which was made from something, ketchup, pizza, I don't know. He said, Tell me. He was getting angry. I didn't care if he was angry. He had every reason to be angry. It was an accident, I said.

My father's dirty underthings were always all over the house. There was nowhere to go except for my bedroom, where his dirty underthings were not. So one day I collected all of his dirty underthings in a bag. And I took the bag out to the yard. And I shook the bag out onto the grass. It looked absurd, all those dirty underthings all over the yard. But it made me laugh for a second, the utter absurdity of this.

I slept better when my boyfriend slept on the couch. That night I had slept straight through the night. But in the morning a bird flew in through the bedroom window. It was filthy, circling, crashing crazy into the walls. I was screaming for my boyfriend to help. I felt dumb screaming for help. I felt dumb screaming at all. The bird left streaks of dark on the ceiling. Feathers popped out from its wings. The bird is not a metaphor. It's not meant to symbolize anything. It was just a bird.

I should say there was one puzzle I never solved as a kid. In it, a hotel has an infinite number of rooms. There is someone staying in each of the rooms. Then an infinite number of people walk in. They each want a room, and, though the rooms are filled, they each get one. The question, of course, is how.

I picked at the red dots on the table. They came up from the table in perfect circles. My brother said, Stop that. I said, Stop what. He pointed to my hands. He said, Stop that. It was like he was the one older and I was the one younger. It was like he was tough and I was not. I said, Where's your girl. He said, She's not my girl. There was no reason to talk about the girl. She was trash like all of the girls. I said, She wouldn't fuck you. He said, Yeah, right. I said, Yeah, right. She wouldn't fuck you, I said. Then my brother slammed his fist into the table. The crumbs on the table jumped, and I would have laughed if things had been different. But I didn't like how my brother was acting. He was trying to act tough. And he looked tough. But that didn't mean he was tough. He said, Tell me the truth. I said, What truth. I said, I told you the truth. I said, There is no truth. But what did I know about truth. I was only fucking around. And my brother knew I was fucking around. So he reached across the table. He grabbed my arm. He squeezed too hard. He said, Tell me the truth. I said, Let me go. But he squeezed my arm harder. I hadn't thought he could squeeze it harder. I could feel the bone in my arm. I could feel the bone about to snap. He said, Tell me the truth. I said, Let me go. I felt like I would cry. But I was not the type of girl to cry. So I said, He hit me in the face with a book.

Several times, my father threw the dolls into the trash. And my brother would find the dolls in the trash, clean them up, and stand them, again, on his dresser. Then my father would sit my brother at the kitchen table. Boy, he would say. You are not your father's son, he would say. No one will save you, he would say. There's no great man in the clouds, he would say. And my brother would get this look on his face. It was the same dumb look he often got. Though at that one point I did see brightness. I never told this to my father. That I saw brightness at that one point.

My father had been dying for a very long time. It was something with his lungs. They sounded like a storm. They were going to stop working, we had been told. We waited years for them to stop working. And when they did stop working, he called my brother and said, Pray for me, boy. Then he called me and said, Pray for me, girl. But neither of us knew how to pray.

My brother said, He hit you with a fucking book. I said, Yes. I said, No. He said, Which. He said, Yes or no. It was an accident, I said. An accident, he said. Bullshit, he said. There are no accidents, he said. Bullshit, I said. There are only accidents, I said.

The bird was crashing into the walls. I got out of bed. I took a book from a shelf. I waved the book around. I swatted the bird through the window. I walked out of the bedroom. I was still holding the book in the hallway. I was still holding the book, in the room in which my boyfriend was sleeping on the couch. And I was still holding the book standing over my boyfriend as he slept. And I stood there, still, still holding the book, as he opened his eyes, looking terrified.

I don't know what I was thinking. Perhaps I wasn't thinking. Perhaps I was only feeling. Perhaps I was feeling like a guy. And what does that mean. I don't know what that means.

My brother let go of my arm and slammed his fist again into the table. And when the crumbs on the table jumped this time, it wasn't funny. I stood and said, Fuck this. I said, I'm going. And my brother said, Where are you going. I said, I'm going somewhere. And my brother laughed. He said, You're going nowhere.

Once, I was bigger than my brother. And I knew he would one day be bigger than I was. And I knew that once he was bigger than I was, he always would be bigger. Because I would not get bigger than I was. But I would always be the bigger prick. Because I was the biggest prick I knew.

I watched from my bedroom window as my father found his underthings all over the yard. I could tell he was angry by the way he stomped toward the house. And by the sound the door made. And by the weight of his steps in the hallway. Then I heard him open my brother's door. Then I heard my brother's voice. I heard my brother's body hit the wall.

And did I try to stop my father. I suppose I did not. I suppose I had my reasons for letting him throw my brother around.

At some point, my father moved away. We were older then, and he moved to another city. He moved to the city for a woman. And then he left that woman. And then there was a second woman. And then he left that woman too. And then there was a third. And then he left that woman. And then there was a fourth. After he died, we met the fourth. She called herself your father's friend. She told us things we had to do. There were people to meet and people to pay. There were papers to sign and objects to put into boxes. And when every last paper had been signed and every last object had been boxed, she drove us to the airport in her very big car and sad music played and she told us she prayed for our father. And on any other day, we would have laughed. We would have told her what he told us. That no one will save you. That there's no great man in the clouds.

And on the plane going home, we were very happy. Our father had died, and we had been terribly sad. But on the plane going home, I don't think we had ever been that happy. We were so happy we were going home, we would not have cared if the plane had crashed. We drank whiskey out of tiny bottles. We spent all our money on the whiskey. We were drunk and we were fucking happy. And when the plane landed, we were still laughing. It was probably something not even funny. It was probably something pretty dark. We probably shouldn't have been laughing at all. But we were still laughing waiting for our bags. Some of the bags were our father's bags. These bags were filled with our father's things. They were coming around with the other bags. One of them had a dent in it. One of them had a stain. And then we were no longer laughing. We were no longer happy but just absurdly sad.

My brother smoked his first cigarette at the kitchen table. He was ten and the cigarette was unfiltered, and he took a long drag, and my father said, Boy, and my father was proud. And when my brother started choking, my father laughed his ass off, and I laughed my ass off too. My brother just looked so dumb, not able to stop that choking. He looked so dumb, the smoke just pouring out of his dumb head, my brother, who was not my father's son.

I was standing over my boyfriend. It had started to rain. And I liked, in that moment, the rain. I mean I liked, in that moment, the sound of the rain. And I liked the weight of the book in my hand. But it must have seemed like a night terror to him. It must have seemed like a dream of being killed. Because in seconds my boyfriend was off the couch. Then he was the one holding the book.

We were standing at the kitchen table. We were playing the dumb parts we played. It was like I was trying to play a woman, and he was trying to play a man. It was like I was trying to play the victim, and he was trying to play the savior. He said, I'm going to kill him. I said, Then kill him. But my brother would not kill my boyfriend. Because he was my brother, not my father. And so my brother would stand at the kitchen table. And I would stand at the kitchen table. And eventually, my brother would go to his job. He would pick up weights. He would haul out trash. But for now, he was going nowhere. And I was going nowhere. For now, we were putting on a show. It was a show we put on for each other. It was a show we put on for our father. It was a show we put on for our mother. It was utterly absurd, our show. Just a little girl playing little girl. Just a big guy playing big guy. And who was the girl. And who was the guy. It was so confusing, our show. We didn't always stick to our lines. We didn't always know our lines.

I should have started with this: A bird flew into the bedroom. And followed with: It was flying crazy into the walls. Feathers floated from the ceiling. I swatted at the bird with a book. I swatted it back through the window.

I should have started with this: I was standing in the hallway. And followed with: I was standing over my boyfriend's sleeping body. I wasn't thinking as I stood over his body. I was just hold-ing a book up high while he slept.

One morning my father threw my brother's dolls into the trash. And this time he locked the trash in the trunk of his car. And this time my brother cried all morning, and my father didn't know what to do. At some point they had a private talk. My father was sitting on my brother's bed. My brother was crying on the floor. I was standing in the doorway. Boys only, my father said, and slammed the door in my face. I suddenly felt like the only person in the world. I felt like I was standing on the moon. I screamed, Fuck you, at the door. I screamed, Fuck you, and kicked the door. I screamed, Fuck you pricks, and kicked a hole right through the fucking door.

Later that day, my father took us for pizza. And after we ate our pizza, he took us to a toy store. It was the biggest toy store in the city. My father bought me a book on puzzles. He bought my brother a rocket to build. My brother, for whom there was still hope. He could still become an astronaut.

My brother smoked his second cigarette at the kitchen table. He smoked his third cigarette at the kitchen table. He smoked his fourth, and it was terrible to watch him smoke. It was abso-lutely brutal. But did I try to stop him. He was so determined. I couldn't stop him.

And did I try to stop my boyfriend as the book was rushing to-ward my face. Let's just say I was working through something. I was making up for something.

This had nothing to do with my mother. When I stood at the mirror, I did not see my mother's face. It was not that at all. My mother was not a banged-up woman. She was a brilliant woman. She left the house. And I could not have stopped her.

Just before he died, my father came back to the city for business. We met him at a trashy bar. He looked old. He could barely talk. He coughed the whole night. Everyone knew he was going to die. The bartender gave him water. She gave him a look. She gave us all that look. And my father grabbed the bartender's arm and pulled her in toward him. And through all his coughing, he was able to say something to her. I don't know why I thought he would say something nice, like thank you or something like that. It wasn't like he was that type. He did not say something nice. He said something about her body. Something about her ass. Her amazing ass. My father said to me, Look at that ass. I looked at the bartender's face. It was alarming how much she hated us. And my boyfriend snapped at my father for this. And my brother snapped at my boyfriend. And I snapped at my brother. And as the bartender walked away, my brother looked at her ass. And my boyfriend looked at her ass. And I, as well, looked at her ass. And it was amazing.

There was a night my boyfriend waked me, screaming. Then he was rushing through the room, and I was screaming too. Then he was in the hallway, then at the door, then running down a flight of stairs, and I was running after him, screaming, Don't. Outside were cars and people on the street. My boyfriend ran out, screaming, They want me. I screamed, No one wants you. He screamed, Yes they do. Then he was running into traffic.

Then I was running too. Then someone else screamed. Tires screeched. I grabbed my boyfriend's arm.

Next we were standing on the sidewalk. People were staring at my boyfriend. My boyfriend asked how he had gotten there. I guess he meant to the sidewalk. But either way, I did not have an answer. Because it was just too huge a question. Because it was probably a miracle. I mean how the fuck did I get there. How did anyone get there on that street. Some miraculous spark that just kept on. I knew nothing about miracles. I was not the one to ask. But I knew how to get my boyfriend up the stairs.

I could have solved that puzzle at any point. It was a nothing puzzle to solve. But I waited years to solve it. Because I did not want to solve it. A hotel with an infinite number of rooms. I just loved the thought of that hotel. Just imagine that hotel.

Look. What if there was no bird. What if there was no bird flying through the room. What if there was only me and the book. What if I made up the bird.

And what if I was holding the book like this. And what if I was standing there like this. And what if I made a face like this. And what if I felt like a zombie. And what if I felt like an animal. And what if I felt just like a guy. And what if he opened his eyes like this. What if he looked at me like this. I said to my brother, You have never seen terror like this.

I should have started with this: After my boyfriend hit me in the face with the book, everything stopped. And followed with:

UNDERTHINGS

I mean the rain and every blade of grass and every leaf on every tree and air and light and time and

I should have started with this: After my boyfriend hit me in the face with the book, everything started. And followed with:

I should say there were good times with my boyfriend. The morning after he ran to the street, we laughed pretty hard. We laughed at his saying, They want me. And at my saying, No one wants you. And we laughed at the sound the tires made. And at the person who screamed. And at his dumb-as-shit questions. And my dumb-as-shit answers. We laughed pretty much all morning.

But one day I would be at my brother's again. I would have another mark on my face. The mark would be on the same side as the other mark. But it would be flatter than the other mark. It would not be from a book this time. And I would know something then that I hadn't, before that day, known.

And on that day, as my brother stood to leave, I would tell him the unsolved puzzle. I would hope that he would solve it. I would hope his brilliance would return. I didn't want my brother to be my father. I wanted him to be my mother. The question, I would say to him, is how. How, I would say, but he wouldn't care. He would leave his place. He would find my boyfriend. And I would sit there, waiting.

But before that day was this day, and it seemed the rain would never stop.

And streets would flood and bridges would fall and people would die, and no one ever predicted all that rain.

And did you want to hit him, my brother said.

I was not that type of girl.

I was my father's daughter, not my father.

I didn't hit him, I said.

And the rain would fall for thirty days, and it seemed the rain would never stop.

But did you want to hit him, my brother said.

And a day would come that would be the last.

Not the last of the rain, but the last of the days.

And no great man would come to save us.

No great man would ever come.

And I would hold up my hand for a high five.

And my brother would hold up his.

UNIVERSE

One does not start with mourning doves.

One cannot start with doves surrounding the bedroom.

One starts with the trip to Sausalito, the quick ride over the bridge, the city shrinking in the side-view.

One starts with the trip, as the details of the trip are simple: Mexican food, espresso.

The details are simple: houseboats and the theater where one remembered seeing a film on a first date, a blind date, some years back.

The date himself, one remembered, was beautiful, the night itself, and if one felt to sleep with him on the first date, one would have gotten, one would guess, the second date.

The film was foreign, fine, two perfect people falling in love.

One cannot start with mourning doves surrounding the bedroom, several in windows sitting on branches, making their hollow sound.

One cannot start with doves looking through the windows to where one lay in one's bed, still, too late to be lying still in one's bed.

One starts with something lighter, light, the Mexican food,

the espresso, and, walking past the theater, one told one's friend about the blind date from years back, how beautiful his face was; how sentimental the film; how one fell for it, still, the perfect people falling in love; how after the date, one went back to his place; how one was asked to take off one's shoes; how one was asked to lie in his bed; how one did not go all the way on first dates; how that was back then; how this was now.

One's friend laughed, and all that mattered, in this moment, was this moment.

All that mattered in the next moment was the pulling in one's gut as one laughed too.

One mentions the pulling as it too is a detail, the detail that made one stay in one's bedroom, shades drawn, the following day and the following day, but it was a great day, this day, to be on the other side of the bridge.

Everything was a metaphor this day.

Like the bridge itself.

Like the lack of traffic on the bridge.

Like the doves cooing from every branch that morning in bed, and one read the doves as a sign of something to come.

One was right to do so; everything that day was a sign.

Not from the universe, as one now knows the universe is not in control, as one now knows the universe is not calling the shots, as one now knows that neither is there human control and neither is there fate and neither is there an explanation for what there is.

There is just the endless dialogue between one's own soft brain and one's own soft brain.

One has to accept this.

It was just a morning.

It was just a visit one had to get to, and as the birds flew off the branches, one by one, one got out of bed, one pulled on clothes, one left.

It was just the usual: one's body transported as if pulled by strings.

Then the wait, feet up, for the doctor to enter, the doctor who called one Baltimore; How's it going, Baltimore, he'd say, and laugh.

After, one felt the need to leave the city, to see it shrinking in the side-view.

And when one felt like being alone, one left one's friend at the table, one stood outside in the wind, looking toward the houseboats, feeling half-pathetic, half-heroic.

Which is to say half-oneself, half–someone else.

Once back inside, one didn't explain the events of outside, that while one's hair was whipping about the way one would imagine, there was a pulling in one's gut.

One only said one saw the houseboats, a man in a straw hat standing on one, sweeping its floor, and this seemed a metaphor too.

But for what.

One does not know.

Perhaps something about out with the old.

Perhaps something about each man for himself.

Perhaps something about that.

The story itself is a force inside; the doctor afraid to move closer; one's insides afloat, quivering black and white on a screen.

The doctor said nothing, kept his distance.

One knew what he was thinking.

One now was fluent in the doctor's face.

One now was fluent in one's insides.

One now knew where to find this and that: the cord, the head, the spastic flicker of the heart.

When the doctor sighed, looked down, one thought, Now what.

The nurse, as well, looked down.

There was nowhere else to look.

This was not the time for words.

This was not the time to say something dumb.

Anything would have been dumb.

Fuck this would have been dumb.

Why would have been pathetic.

It was supposed to happen to others.

It was not supposed to happen.

One was only trying to be an adult.

One was only trying to start one's life.

One was only trying to start another.

Check again, one said.

One said, Check again.

Check again, one said.

The heart wasn't beating.

One said, Check again.

The doctor held out his hand for a handshake and anyone would have been confused.

It was not a handshake but a way to help one up.

Tomorrow, he said.

One did not want to get up.

The technical term was *aspiration,* and this was not the time to deconstruct words.

Get dressed, Baltimore, he said.

One left him hanging, hand in the air, and he left.

When one's phone rang, one was still undressed, standing barefoot by the screen.

One's friend said, What do you need.

It was too big a question.

There were machines in the room one did not understand.

There were jars of sticks one could not figure out, not the jars, but the sticks.

One's man was supposed to be there, helping to pull one's underwear on.

One's man was supposed to tell one what next.

But there is nothing to say about one's man.

One's man was only in one's mind.

In one's mind he had those long legs one loved and ragged jeans.

He had hair hanging into his eyes.

But this is not about one's man.

Because there was no man.

Forget the man.

There was only one standing alone in a room.

There was one's friend saying, What.

It was too hard a question.

One had a sudden need to be melodramatic.

One had a sudden need to be difficult, loud, one's default before one learned to perform.

Then came the need to be driven fast across the bridge, the need to see water, seabirds, houseboats moored to a dock.

A sign on the wall said to avoid drinking liquor.

A sign on the wall said to avoid eating shark.

But one could now drink heavily.

One could now eat shark.

One would try to remember to say this to one's friend.

I can eat a whole fucking shark, one would say.

But one would quickly forget this joke.

And what good is it, sitting here now.

One stayed undressed until the nurse knocked on the door, knocked again, said one's name, knocked again, opened the door still saying one's name, still knocking.

The menu said the espresso was the best in Sausalito, and, not having tried it elsewhere, one believed it was.

The Mexican food, too, one feels was the best.

One liked to see the theater again.

To be reminded that one cannot force a spark in another.

That one can get undressed, get into his bed, and still get sent home in a cab.

That one can watch a sunrise by oneself on one's living room floor, a perfect cliché.

That one can make decisions about one's future on one's living room floor, as the sun moves from chair to couch to wall.

And the silent melodrama of this.

One used to think *mourning* was spelled *morning,* and then, as *morning,* it was a different kind of dove, a different sound they made.

That was in Baltimore, and then one was young and one was dumb.

And then one thought one was tough.

And that was then, and everything then was Baltimore Baltimore Baltimore.

And the brilliance of this.

Now though.

This is the West.

This is what it is to be an adult.

And one cannot handle the accuracy of these birds.

One cannot handle the sentimental fuckload that is these birds.

One cannot even write these birds without feeling like one of those people one detests.

One of what people.

You know what people.

But this is not the time to detest those people.

This is not the time to detest oneself.

This was not a thing one could control.

Because one was never in control.

Because nothing was ever in control.

The technical term was *spontaneous.*

The technical term was *involuntary.*

There was no explanation.

There was only rising as if pulled by strings.

There was only wondering what next.

And never knowing what next.

The café would close and the ride back to the city was looming.

There would first be a joke about cigarettes, about picking up smoking.

There would first be a joke about whiskey, about drinking oneself sick, about drinking oneself under the fucking table.

There would first be the hope that one's friend would head the car north instead, along the coast, that one would never return.

But one's friend needed to get back to the city.

One's friend had a wife, kids, waiting on the other side of the bridge.

For one's friend, there was dinner waiting, warm, and talk of the safe and dull events of a day.

And for one there was night, then later night.

And the melodrama that was a ceiling coming into view.

And the melodrama that was one's brain considering the ceiling.

And the sudden deep thoughts one had that only seemed deep, that only seemed sudden.

About each man for himself.

About out with the old.

And so on and so on.

Listen to this, friend.

One had it going on in Baltimore.

One was never safe, never dull.

One had different aspirations.

But that was then, and now a new city forced its way through the windshield.

And one could pretend one was tough, still.

One could pretend one could handle it all.

One could say, Beautiful, and point to the skyline.

One could pretend one had never fallen in love.

With a brilliant thought.

A faceless man.

A rapid flicker on a screen.

It's all heart at this point, the doctor once said, and shook one's hand.

And one could laugh out the window, not one of those people, not one of those sentimental fucks, and pretend one's own heart hadn't stopped.

COWGIRL

; it was virtual, the killing; it was conference call, the killing; it was party line, a party; it was everyone talking at once; it was everyone talking and me in charge; it was nearing morning, almost light; it was the doctor begging me, Come on already; it was the doctor begging me, Do it already; it was me saying, You do it already; it was my brother laughing into his phone; it was my mother sighing into hers; it was my mother saying, This isn't funny; it was my mother saying, You kids are monsters; it was my mother saying, I'm hanging up; it was the voice she used when we were kids; we hated that voice when we were kids; my father hated that crazy voice; he called her crazy with that voice; he called her crazy, that way she got; it was his fault she was crazy; it was his fault everything went the way it did; it was his fault everything in the world; but it was too easy to blame the father; I was done with blaming the father; I would take the blame from this point on; I would take the blame for the world how it was; the world was in a state of collapse; the world was collapsing in my hands; the world was my mother and the voice we hated as kids; it was my brother saying to my mother, Take a fucking pill; it was my mother laughing too hard now; it was my brother laughing again; it was funny because we were on the phone; it was funny because we were in different rooms on different streets in different states; it was funny because it wasn't funny; it was funny because it was nothing even close to funny; but it was totally ours; it was no one else's but stupid ours: like words you made up as kids, like things you watched through a keyhole as kids; it was my TV on when it shouldn't have been; it was my brother saying, Turn down the fucking TV; it was me saying, No fucking way; it was my brother saying, This is serious shit; it was me thinking, You don't know serious shit; it was rain for the tenth day in a row; it was twelve spiders in twelve corners in three rooms in the house; it was a different time zone where I was; it was a different altogether time; it was the doctor saying, I need you to focus; it was never just, I need you; it was never just, Let's have a good time; it was the doctor saying, I need you to pull the plug; it was never that; it was softer than that; it was more like, I need you to do the right thing; it was more like, Your father would want it this way; it was me not knowing what he would want; it was no one knowing what anyone else would ever want: even if he said it to your face, even if he wrote it down, even if he carved it into a tree, into the sidewalk, into the softest part of your arm; it was the doctor saying, This isn't funny; it was the doctor saying, This isn't life; it was the doctor saying, Trust me; it was hard to trust a person I couldn't see; it was hard to trust a person I could; it was like watching through a keyhole as a kid; it was long ago that one day; it was no big deal that one day; it was no big deal, looking in at him; it was no big deal, walking in on them; my father screamed; the lady screamed; my mother was out of town; I called her; she came back to town; she kicked him out; the end; it wasn't the thing that did me in; it was the conference call that did me in; it was the conference

call why I had issues; and here I was on a date in a bar; here I was
on a date with a guy and I told him there was no way; here I was
in a lovely skirt, my knees exposed, his hand about to touch my
knee, and I told him no fucking way; now was always no fucking way; now was always no fucking; now was the luxury of
years passed; now was the luxury of the bartender's serious face;
now was his serious eyes as he described this wine or that; and it
was me drinking way too much; it was the date saying, I think
you've got issues; it was me saying, I think everyone's got issues;
it was the date saying, I think you know what I mean; it was me
saying, Bartender; it was the date saying, What's your deal; it
was me saying, There's no deal; it was no big deal, my deal; it
was too easy to blame the father; it was too easy to blame a
father dying on a terrible narrow bed I never saw; it was stupid
to blame a terrible plug I never saw; it was unclear if the plug
was a literal plug or not; it was possibly a switch one flipped; it
was possibly a metaphor; but it was easier to say a plug; because
it was something I never saw, the plug; it was virtual, the plug;
and it was virtual, the terrible narrow bed; and it was virtual, the
father; and it was crazy how he got that way; it was crazy that
way he got; it was clichéd that way he got; it was too many
drinks; it was too many pills; it was rock star how he was; it was
hotel room how it was; it was calling me in the night; it was
singing stupid songs to my machine; it was, Wake up little, etc.;
it was, Wake up little, etc.; it was never funny; and then he got
sick; and then he got sicker, and then, and then; it was never
once funny; it was never me laughing; it was me looking for the
bartender; it was another round; it was another round; it was me
feeling slightly better; it was a shame, of course, ever feeling better; it was the worst shame ever, killing one's father; it was the
worst shame ever, really killing him really; it was the worst shame

ever, the virtual way I did; it was me lying on my bed; it was me
and the phone pressed to my ear; it was me watching some actor
on TV; it was some familiar face that shouldn't have been familiar; it was my brother and mother in my head; it was all the voices
I didn't want in my head; it was all the voices telling me to do the
right thing; it was all the voices somehow knowing the right
thing, and I didn't even know the exact time; because there was
no such thing as exact time; because it was one time where I was,
one time where they were, one time where he was; it was me saying, Wait a second; it was me saying, Just wait a fucking second;
it was me saying, Just shut up a fucking second; it was wrong to
say this to my family; it was only an actor on TV; it was only the
actor saying something funny; it was only the actor saying a
really funny joke; it was me needing a really funny joke right
then; it was a shame to need a joke right then; it was me waiting,
everyone yelling; it was me about to laugh my ass off; it was my
mother complaining weeks later; it was my mother complaining,
You shouldn't have called me; it was my mother complaining,
You put me in a hard place; it was my mother complaining, He
was a monster; it was me thinking, Who put who in a hard place;
it was me saying, Who put who; it was me saying, You had me;
it was me saying, You put me in the worst hard place: the older
kid, the only girl; I said, Who put who; she said, Who put whom;
I said, Exactly; my father put me in a hard place; my father put
my mother in a hard place; my father put the lady in a hard
place; my eye was pressed to a hard place; my father put the lady
in front of him; he stuck her there in front of him; she was
younger than my mother; it was a hard place to be; it was probably love; it was probably total love; it was her laugh that waked
me; it was her stupid laugh; and there was no keyhole; it was
only a metaphor, I think; it was only me opening the door, I

think; it was only me screaming, I think now, something awful; it was my father screaming something too; and it was me screaming something else; and it was shameful, the lady screaming something too; it was shameful how trashy, just screaming like that; it was shameful being a lady like that; it was my brother hiding in his room; it was my mother out of town; it was my mother still able to dream something lovely; it was my mother about to dream something lovely; it was me running out to the lawn; it was me standing under some dumb moon not knowing what next: like maybe I could run away, like maybe if I were a guy, like maybe if I were that girl; but I went back inside; and it wasn't the beginning of the end; it was the beginning of something else; her purse was on the hallway floor; and it was my floor, that hallway floor; meaning it was my purse on the hallway floor; meaning it was my stuff in that purse: meaning her comb, meaning her ten dollars, meaning her ID; it was the beginning of the beginning; I deserved something that night too; and her picture looked nothing like me; and her name was impossible to pronounce; and I memorized the spelling of her name; and I memorized her address; and I figured out her sign; and I styled my hair to look like hers; and I made a face that looked like hers; and the ID worked for many years; meaning I was a piece of trash for many years; I was a piece of trash walking into bars; it was me before I had issues; it was me before no fucking way; it was me before no fucking; it was me before, I'm too fucked up; it was the date giving that look dates gave; it was me thinking, Try killing yours, motherfucker; it was me saying, Drink your drink, motherfucker; it was just shut up shut up shut up; it was a shame to make a virtual decision; it was a shame pulling a virtual plug; it was a shame my ear pressed to a hard place; it was only voices in my head; it was only some actor on

TV; it was half my brain waiting for the punch line; it was half my brain pulling a plug from a wall; it was pulling the plug in my brain like a pro; it was swinging the cord like a lasso; it was me like a cowgirl, swinging the cord around my head; it was the date saying, You've got issues; it was the date saying, Serious ones; it wasn't always like this though; it was a good time with that ID; I was a good time with that ID; I met guys and it was a good time back then; it was the ID getting me in; it was the ID getting me what I wanted; though there was a night a bouncer said, ID; I looked around like no big deal; there was a guy in the bar I liked; the bouncer looked at my ID; he said, What's your name; he said, Where do you live; he said, What's your sign; I was ready for this; I was well rehearsed; I said, Virgo; he said, No way; he said, You're a Capricorn; he said, And a liar; it was true; I was a Capricorn; I was also a liar; the whole point of the story is something else; the whole point is I wasn't always this pent up; the whole point is I wasn't always; I said, You caught me; the bouncer said, Get out of here; he said, Liar; he said, Get; but I wanted to go into the bar; I said, Come on; I touched his leg; I said, I'm a Capricorn; I said, You guessed it; I couldn't hide what I was; I said, I'll buy you a drink; he shifted; his leg was too warm; another bouncer walked up; then there were too many men in the picture; then there were too many men I needed to please; there were often too many men; some nights I just wanted to kiss the softest part of my arm; some nights I just wanted to think of some guy I thought I loved; some nights I waked, my mouth still pressed to my arm; some nights I could stay there and fall back into dreams; some nights, though, the phone rang through the night; some nights were songs on my machine; some nights were rain on my machine; some nights were dead air on my machine; some nights I should have said, No no no;

some nights I should have fallen back into my arm; I was in love with myself some nights; but there were often too many men in the picture; there were often too many men I needed to please; and there was no way to shut it off; there was the date wanting something I didn't want; there was my father singing, Wake up wake up; there was the doctor saying, Do it already; there was my brother saying, Do it already; there was a plane past the window; there was sun past the window; and there was me saying, Mother, to nothing there; there was me saying, Mother, but she had hung up; because nothing was left but, Shut it off; because nothing was left but, Do it already; then it was a hum from some machine gone dead; then everything went dead; all the voices in my head went dead; then the plane; then the sun; then light; then air; then the punch line to the actor's joke; then another joke; then another joke;

SPECTACLE

When the plane crashed, I was all messed up.

For years, I was all messed up.

I could see the scene inside the plane.

I could see the scene outside.

And I had thoughts of flying.

Then thoughts of falling.

Then thoughts of crashing to the ground.

There was a time I thought of other things.

I could become so gripped by things.

Like for a time I thought of underwater.

I mean I was gripped by thoughts of being underwater.

Because my father once said, when I shouldn't have been listening, What if all the earth's water were drained.

Because my father once said, when I was too young to deal with it, It would be wild.

He said there'd be ships and planes and cars and bodies.

It made me afraid for years.

I was afraid to drive across bridges.

I was afraid the bridges would collapse.

Then the car would sink.

The car would slowly fill with water.
And my body would fill until it burst.
For years I would replay this scene.
Until there was another scene.
And then it was this other scene.
And the words they used to describe it.
And the girl I knew who was in it.
She was coming back from study abroad.
I was not allowed to study abroad.
This is not the time to talk about this.
This is not the time to talk about me.
But my father was to blame for this.
My father preferred I went nowhere.
And I went nowhere for many years.
At some point I got over it.
Because at some point I had no choice.
Because one gets older and one has places one needs to be.
So I bought a ticket to be somewhere.
It doesn't matter where I was going.
What matters is I was on a plane.
I was in the air.
The flight attendant was at my row.
Her skirt made a sound like paper.
She said, Are you all right.
I knew I didn't seem all right.
And I knew it was wrong not to seem all right.
Because my father was often not all right.
And I took after him in many ways.
No one wanted to see the ways in which I did.
So I pressed my face to the window.
I could see our shadow on the backs of clouds.

It was perfectly plane shaped, our shadow.
And as we went higher,
And when our shadow was smallest,
And when there was no shape, but just a point,
And when there was no point,
The flight attendant said, Are you all right.
She was wearing too much makeup.
It was orange and stopped where the face stopped being a face.
There was a time I wore too much makeup.
It was sophomore year I wore too much.
It was part of my performance then.
I was not a nice girl.
I was a very nice girl.
I was not very nice.
There was a way I was.
There was what I wore.
And I danced wildly for the guys I liked.
I danced obscenely one could say.
I was just a bit obscene back then.
By which I mean my needs were just a bit obscene.
It was something one didn't fully get over.
It was something that came from being a girl.
So there was no point in her asking, Are you all right.
The right thing to ask was, How can I help you.
The right thing to ask was, What can I get you.
The right thing to ask was, What exactly do you need.
It was hard to know exactly what I needed.
There were too many things going on.
There was my body inside a plane.
There was my mind inside my body.
And the mess of that.

Listen.

Sophomore year was years before.

I hung out with the girl back then.

She had two blond streaks.

Her initials were G.O.D.

I thought at first she would be too cool.

But she was not, as it turned out, too cool.

She was cool, but it turned out I was too.

Because I knew how to be from watching girls.

And I knew, as well, from watching guys.

There was a way they stood there.

And the girls just stood there.

And what they wore.

We knew what to wear.

We wore schoolgirl skirts from the Goodwill.

We wore guy's sweaters and black tights.

The Goodwill was on the corner of North and Harford, and no one wanted to be there.

People went there because they were either poor or cool.

The poor people bought serious clothing.

We watched a woman buy a wedding dress there.

We weren't laughing as she held the dress up to herself.

We weren't laughing that she was by herself and holding up this tattered, yellowed dress.

We were poor too, but we were not the kind of poor that counted as poor.

We were the other kind, the student kind.

We were the kind that bought shit fast, then ran up North.

North was dangerous for girls like us.

There were no trees.

There was endless brick.

There was broken glass.

There were car alarms.

There were guys who wanted to fuck you up.

They wanted to get you hooked on things.

We were already hooked on things.

We weren't hooked, but we were something like it.

The guys said, Sister.

They said, Let's see that smile.

They said, Let's see that ass.

They said, You make me hard.

We said, Fuck you.

We had other guys.

We had guys we liked.

They were students like us.

They lived in small apartments like us.

They took useless classes like us.

We took philosophy because they took it too.

Though we didn't understand philosophy.

We passed notes in class on how bored we were.

And how hungry we were.

How over it we always were.

Nights, we all went to the bar.

We got fucked up and stood around.

There was a guy at the bar we didn't like.

He called himself the mystic.

He wore a hat made of old socks sewn together.

He was an asshole, this guy, and only he called himself the mystic.

We called the guy the misfit.

He would put himself into a trance.

We called the trance the so-called trance.

We tried to ignore him when he rolled his eyes back into his head.

We said, So what, when he predicted things that didn't matter.

Like what song would come on.

Or who would walk through the door.

And the misfit would say some shit to us.

Like fuck you or something.

And the girl and I would laugh.

But this was years before and who cares about this asshole.

Let me get back to the subject.

Let me get the subject back.

The flight attendant.

I have lost her orange face.

I have lost the papery sound of her skirt.

And the look she gave.

She needed me to seem all right.

And I wanted to seem all right.

But I was thinking the scene I often thought.

And thinking the words they used.

They described it as a fireball.

They described it as a spectacle.

I didn't know how to deal with it then.

I tried to deal with it then.

I tried to deal with it by going nowhere.

That was my father's joke.

I would stop by on my way to class.

I would bring him things to eat.

I would watch him lying on the couch.

I would stand there waiting for something.

I was always waiting for something.

And my father would say, Get over it.

You need to get over it, he would say.

You need to get over her, he would say.

Then, Where are you going, he would say, as I turned to leave.

Nowhere fast, he would say, as I opened the door.

He would laugh his ass off from the couch.

He loved his joke.

But the real joke was I would return to him.

And I would return again.

I would return again.

Until there was nothing to return to.

Just my father's empty house.

It was then I bought a ticket.

I got my body onto a plane.

I got my mind into my body.

I was trying to prove something, I suppose.

But earlier, in the airport, I thought to turn back.

I was afraid and thought to go back.

So when a guy said, Do you need help, I said, Yes.

He was missing a tooth, and I never liked to see this.

It reminded me of something from when I was a kid, a guy or something I shouldn't have seen, and then, as a kid, it made me sad.

Though it should have been funny when I was a kid, some guy on North just lying there all fucked up.

It should have been funny, some broken guy on a flattened box, a guy my father and I saw on our way to the house.

My father thought it was funny.

Some guy more broken than we could ever be.

More messed up than we could ever be.

My father and I stepped over this guy.

My father laughed.

We walked into the house.

And when the guy in the airport said, How can I help, I said, I don't know.

He said, I can carry your bag, and I said, I can carry my bag.

He said, What do you need, and I said, I need a lot of things.

I need help, I said.

I'm in need, I said.

I reached for his arm.

He said, I can carry your bag.

There are too many guys in this story.

For a story about a girl, that is.

For a story about being a girl, that is.

This guy was missing a tooth, and nobody cares.

The guy on North, nobody cares.

My father, please.

And the guy from the bar.

He was not a mystic.

There are no mystics.

There are people who know shit and people who don't.

And the people who know shit only know shit because they're watching.

And the people who don't only don't because they're not.

The night before she left we'd gone to the bar.

And the girl and I were dancing.

And the mystic was watching us dance.

And a guy I liked was watching us dance.

I can remember feeling a certain way.

I felt like a star.

Like an actual star.

Like just before the supernova.

And I wanted time to stop right there.

It was obscene, I know, to want time to stop.

Obscene to love this hard a specific point in time.

But it was more obscene that one couldn't stop it.

That no one really was in charge.

The flight attendant couldn't save me.

She couldn't even save herself.

Not in the event of a spectacle.

We would all just be the spectacle.

So the right thing to ask was, How could one possibly be all right.

I had no answer.

I have no answer now.

When I asked if I could study abroad, my father laughed and said, No way.

He said, Get lost.

And how terrible not getting what I wanted.

Terrible the cigarette stuck to my father's lip.

The windows like a mean face behind him.

He was still fucked up from the night before.

And I stood there for a while thinking he might change his mind.

But eventually he put out his cigarette.

He fell asleep on the couch.

I left and walked to class.

And the guys on North said, Sister.

They said, Come back here.

They said, Come back.

They said, Come back.

And so what if I had.

Class that day was so boring.

I didn't understand philosophy.

There was no point in understanding.

I just sat there thinking what I often thought.

The bridge collapsing.

The car sinking.

Water rushing in through cracks.

I was going nowhere.

The girl was on her own.

I would tell her after class.

You're on your own, I would say.

And the look on her face.

There are better things to think about.

Like dancing the night before she left.

We were all fucked up, and I felt like a star.

And the guy I liked would spin me around.

And we would leave the bar and go for a ride.

I would tell him, Drive fast, and he would.

Then one thing, another.

My head in his lap.

His hand on my head.

I was too nice a girl.

I was not a nice girl.

I was my father's daughter.

And what does that even mean.

For a long time after, I watched the sky.

It was the sun and it was the moon.

It was birds flying in the shape of a V.

It was clouds in the shapes of everything else.

And nothing happened, except once.

That day I was in class.

I was sitting alone by a window.

I heard the plane before I saw it.
I heard the roar it made.
I heard the roar get louder.
It sounded like something broken.
Or like something breaking down.
Then I saw the plane emerge from the clouds.
It was flying sideways.
It was flying too low.
It was coming straight for the window.
I knew no one else was watching.
That I was the only one who cared.
And so I thought some words.
It was like I was praying.
Like I was praying to someone.
Or praying to something.
I was thinking, Please, and, Please, and, Please.
But then the plane just shot across the sky.
The roar died out.
And I was sitting in the classroom.
I was looking out the window.
On some days I imagine the moment just before.
I imagine seeing a flash.
And on some days, I imagine the moment just after.
I imagine the plane as a rain cloud.
I imagine it spinning until it bursts.
Then I imagine flying through clouds.
Then falling through clouds.
And the ground coming closer.
A town growing clearer.
Then the town.
And then.

It doesn't matter.

All that matters is it was night.

And it was cold.

It was night.

And it was cold.

It was night.

And it was cold.

Just stop.

Outside the window now were stars.

And there were lights below, as well.

The flight attendant was waiting for me.

She was waiting for me to be all right.

But I would never be what she needed.

So I had to perform.

I had to lie.

I had to say, I'm all right.

And I forced myself to look all right.

And I forced it harder.

And forced it harder.

Until she went away.

And I'm sorry, but I lied to you too.

When I asked if I could study abroad, my father said, Go.

He said, Get lost.

But I stood there thinking he'd change his mind.

Because I knew I couldn't go.

Because I couldn't leave my father.

I mean I couldn't leave him lying there.

He was more broken than you could ever be.

More messed up than you will ever be.

But there was a time he was all right.

I was a kid, and he took me on a trip.

He took me to the beach.

It was the only trip we ever took.

Days, I swam in the water.

My father sat on the sand.

And on our last day, we watched a sunset.

And my father looked out at the water.

And he said, What if all the earth's water were drained.

And at first I laughed.

But then I thought.

And then I thought.

Listen.

The girl's initials were not G.O.D.

They were just G.D.

I never knew her middle name.

But whatever.

G.D.

G. fucking D.

I am not a mystic.

There are no mystics.

There are people who watch.

And there are people like me.

But that night at the bar, the misfit was on.

He went into his so-called trance.

And he was right about who walked in.

And he was right about every song.

And when he said the girl's name,

And when he reached for her arm,

And when he said, Don't go,

And when I looked at her face,

I should have said something.

I should have done something.

But I was not very nice.
I was not a nice girl.
I just left the bar with the guy I liked.
I told him, Drive fast, and he did.
I'm sorry, but I was my father's daughter.
I did not know how to save you.

SIGNIFIED

Because words are about desire and desire is about the guy who filled my two front tires when one was low. And desire is about the guy who cleaned my windshield as the other, below me, filled.

And there's the guy who pours foam onto my coffee in the shape of a heart and I, each time he pours, so slow, think, Jesus.

Because the guy who pours the foam in the shape of a heart—and I don't know how he does it—is twenty-four, and I am not twenty-four, meaning I am not thirty-four and don't think much of twenty-four except to think I must have been working through something back then, living in that railroad apartment in Baltimore, daydreaming of fame and all that came with fame.

My friends that year said, Why move, but I packed some boxes, crammed the boxes into the car, pushed the couch over the porch. My friends waved from the couch in the rearview mirror and I forgot them once I reached the highway.

Why Boston, they wanted to know.

Because why not.

Or because I imagined Boston as brick-walked and lamp-lit, and I could see myself tromping in boots through the snow.

Or because I imagined a field from a poem I'd read in school as a child.

Or because I had no good answer to, Why Baltimore.

Because I'd gotten held up, a knife point pointing at my face.

All this to say that I remember those friends from then, sitting here now on my new couch, years past, their tattoos I remember of gothic letters and Celtic knot work, their tangled hair. All this to say that I've made a connection, forced as it seems, of twenty-four to twenty-four. I've made a connection of couch to couch. Connections are easy when one is sitting, staring at a wall. There is no deeper meaning. There is no signified.

There is couch and there is couch.

There is the table my feet are on and the table from then. A table we sat at until the pale hum of morning.

There was no such word then as *afterparty.*

There was no such use of the word *random* then, how the kids these days use *random.*

What I mean is the guy who filled my tires looked up and said, of the lowness in one tire and not in the other, Random, and I, remembering running into a curb the night before, driving home from a bar where I sat and sat until giving up, thought, Not really.

And the guy who cleaned the windshield whistled and walked back to the garage.

And the guy who pours the foam into the shape of a heart told my friend of me, She's hot, when my friend went to the café once alone. Your friend, he said, She's hot, and my friend called later to tell me the news.

What was I doing that night. Same thing as this night. Drinking wine. Sitting on the couch, my feet up on the table. These are the clichéd years, these years. The details have been pre-determined. It's a recipe I follow. Very little this, very little that.

I think I said, That's cute. Because that's what one says in this situation. One laughs and says, Cute, and one's friend says, in this situation, You should go for it. Which always seems to mean to me that I should go against something else.

I said, How old is he.

Then I said, That's cute.

Then I said, That's way too young, and my friend, exhaling smoke for emphasis, said, Exactly.

In Baltimore everyone was going for everyone else. Small town. Junkies. We were all the same age, the twenty-somethings, the fifty-somethings. When the bars closed we went to the place that stayed open until morning. Club Midnight. And we drank orange drinks until things felt unreasonable. What was the point of reason. I had no desire for reason. I had only a weak desire—in the words of my shrink from then—to fill a space, and I filled the space. There's a list, somewhere, of the drugs I did. There's a list, somewhere, of who I fucked. I wrote these lists on the backs of napkins, a night at Club Midnight, and everyone thought the lists were too short. Well that was years ago, and things have changed. And there's a list of the drugs I almost did and a list of the guys I almost fucked. And those lists. Believe me. Another story.

So I sat the other night in a bar on a snowy, lamp-lit street, until I realized he—the one I am supposed to desire—my age, a neat haircut, small hands, a tucked-in shirt, a workhorse, a per-fect match—wasn't going to show. Or I realized that he would show and that I would feel disgust. So I stumbled to the car, ended up half the car on the sidewalk, no one around to see it.

I once knew better than to drive.

I mean I once considered other options.

There were no windows in Club Midnight. We knew it was morning because of sudden blue shadows under our eyes. And that shock of light, no matter how pale, when someone opened the door. And the shock of the cold. Jesus. There's no good story to tell except once I decided to wait for the bus. My friends had gone, and I was too sick from drink after drink to drive. Birds were chirping, and I wondered where from. There were no trees. There was nowhere to hide. The man with the knife had a scar on his face and I didn't want a scar on my face. I reached into my pocket, pulled out some ones, and he ran one way, I the other.

And here I am watching the blue turn darker blue behind the trees. And the color of this couch, according to the catalog, is mushroom, which means it's greenish, grayish, brownish. Which means I paid a lot for it. One must pay up when one is following a recipe, and one ingredient is a costly couch. And one is a car. And one is a man. And one is a child.

And one is not thirty-four, though feeling for that warm space in the dimming room.

The men who carried up the couch were older, no-nonsense, beer bellied and smelling of sweat, though had the room been darker, smokier, the bartender filling and filling, the music up high, well, perhaps there'd be something more to say.

The guy filling my tires, when I tried to hand him a few ones, said, No. He said, Jesus, lady, air is free.

And the guy in the café—dark curly hair, that way of dressing—his pants hanging just under his hip bones—blue eyes and so on, the thing with the foam. Well, each time I drop fifty cents into the tip jar, lift my cup, say thank you into the disintegrating heart, never looking up, though I can feel him looking down, and my friend—who always smells like smoke—did I say this—and it's comforting somehow—will say, Aw, a heart, Look, a heart.

And my friend and I will sit on the chairs on the sidewalk out front, even in the cold, and a bus will pass, and the bell on the door will jingle, and the guy will come out, wiping his hands on his pants, lighting a cigarette he pulls from a pale blue box, blowing white smoke into the sky.

And I imagine he's looking at someone else.

And I remember my predestined life. The list of ingredients. And one is a man. And one is a child.

And one is a child.

And I imagine he's looking only at me.

And I imagine the bell sound comes from a horse stopped in the snow at the edge of the woods.

SPECTATOR

; to say I watched him through the keyhole; to say I pressed my
face to the door and watched; to say I had what one could call a
crush; to say the crush was superficial; to say the crush was on
the superficial: like his rib cage through his shirt, like the books
he read and he was brilliant; to say I was not brilliant, though
one day I would be; to say one day I would know my brilliance;
to say one day the world would know my brilliance; and I would
know that day my brilliance made no difference; and I would
know that day no brilliance made a difference; but first I was
mistaken; first I fell for his brilliance; first I fell for his rib cage
through his shirt; to say first I was who I always was; to say I was
always falling incredibly hard; to say I was always falling incredibly hard like women fall; to say I was used to feeling like women
feel; to say I was used to being nothing other than a woman:
which was a good thing, which was not a good thing; and my
shrink would say how in the world was it good to fall incredibly
hard; I didn't always answer her; I was often pulling at threads
at the edge of the chair; I was often staring into the plants and
imagining a jungle; I was often tying my hair into knots and not
untying the knots; to say I had my own things going on; to say

I had my messed-up things I always had; to say I was in that chair for reasons I knew and for reasons I did not; so forgive me, he was my boyfriend's friend; forgive me, he was crashing that night on our couch; forgive me, my boyfriend was out of town; and there's not much to say about my boyfriend; just he was hands down the kindest person I had ever met; just he was hands down the kindest person anyone had ever met; just I had no desire to cheat on him; to say I had no desire to cheat on him again; which is not to say I had no desire; to say we had sat all night on the couch; to say there were important reasons to sit on the couch; to say he had bought important books that day; to say I didn't yet know these important books; and so he was reading to me from one of the books; and so at first I wasn't listening; and so at first I was only looking around the room; and so I will tell you the color of his shirt: black; and I will tell you the color of the couch: red; forgive me for falling for colors; forgive me for falling for someone else's interpretation of colors; to say I was easily seduced; to say I was what one called messed up; to say I was a total fucking mess; to say I was lying back on the couch; and then my legs were over his; and then my eyes were slowly closing; and when I laughed at something, he stopped reading; and when he said, I love your teeth, I laughed again; this is not exactly what happened; to say perhaps I'm making this part up; to say he did not stop reading and say he loved my teeth; to say he did stop reading, but he did not say he loved my teeth; to say he did stop reading, but he said my teeth were crooked; which is to say, at the very least, he was looking at my mouth; which is to say something about love how back then I understood love; and so I opened my eyes; and so I saw him looking at me too hard; and he was not looking at my mouth; to say it was here that I felt a surge; to say it was here that everything shifted; to say it was here that I kicked him in his rib cage; and I was only joking when I kicked him; and he held up the book like a shield; and he was only joking when he held up the book; and my shrink would ask what I meant by *shifted;* and she would ask what I meant by *surge;* and she would ask why I kicked him in his rib cage; and she would ask what happened way back when; she was always asking what happened way back when; I didn't care about way back when; I didn't care about the mystery that was way back; and I would pull at the threads at the edge of the chair; I would tie my hair into knots; I would imagine diving into the jungle at the roots of the plants where I would start a whole new world; I imagined wearing leaves in that world; I imagined tying my hair up in twigs; I imagined I was gigantic; and he was less gigantic; and by *he* I mean every he who ever cast a shadow over me; my shrink did not need to know about the jungle; she did not need to know about the various hes who cast their shadows; my way back when was just clichéd; my way back when was the way back whens of other women in the world; to say there were lines in rooms, and lines were crossed; to say there were rules in rooms, and rules were broken; to say fill in the blanks for yourself; to say fill in the blanks with any words you choose; to say choose the words that happened in your way back; imagine yourself on the couch; imagine he's reading a story to you; imagine the heat of his legs on yours; I can't imagine you would behave as well as I did; I can't imagine you would go to the bedroom, shut the door, lie on the bed, like I did; but the night was over before it should have been over; the night was over, and I thought I would just go to sleep; the night was dead, and I thought I would dream dreams I would forget in the morning; and I whispered something superficial into my pillow; and I whispered something superficial into my arm; and I whispered something desperate into the universe; to say there are no good answers for what one does with desire; to say there is only this constant struggle; to say there is only this constant tugging; to say I wanted to walk back into the room; to say I wanted to go through his suitcase while he slept; to say I wanted to pull something from it; to say I wanted to pull out a shirt and keep it; I would have tried it on over mine; I would have tried it on under mine; this is not about perversion; to say I know what a perversion is; to say it was just a superficial crush; and my boyfriend was hands down fucking perfect; and at some point later that week he came back from out of town; and we were sitting on the couch; and we were looking into each other's bored-as-shit eyes; and I said, Listen, to my boyfriend, and he listened; and I said something funny to my boyfriend, and he laughed; and I said, I could use a drink, and he got me a drink; and he said, I love you; etc.; and he said, I mean it; etc.; and I said something I'm sure I regretted; to say I'm sure I deserved to be punished; to say I'm sure I deserved to be crushed; and I wanted to be punished in the worst way; I wanted to be crushed beneath a hand; my God; I remember a detail from the story he read; to say I remember just one detail: a hot-air balloon, the people in it going higher and higher, the people in it going way too high; and I should say he gave me the book to keep; or I should say I took it from his suitcase; and I should say I was looking for a shirt; or I was looking for a sock; or I was looking for his underwear; and I would have shoved them into my own; and I would have slept all night like that; and I would have dreamed all night like that; and I would have gotten off like that; and this is not some kind of perversion; this is only love how back then I did love; to say one way or another I have the book; to say I could look for it now on a shelf; to say

I could open the book, quote you a line; to say I am very good at seduction; to say I could find a way to keep you awake all night; and I could have kept him awake all night; but on that night I did not: unlike the night I cheated on my boyfriend with my friend, unlike the night I cheated on my boyfriend with his friend, unlike all the nights way back when when everything was just a spark and just a spark; fucking memory; and my shrink would ask why I behaved so well that night; I said I didn't know why; and she said to think; and I said I would think; but I didn't have to think; it was something about the hot-air balloon; and she did not need to know I felt I was in one as he read; she did not need to know I felt twisted loose and shot into space; and I laughed as I was floating away; and when I laughed, he said my teeth were crooked; and I opened my eyes and was looking at his; and of course I felt a surge; and of course it was wrong to feel it; and of course the phone rang right then; and the phone just kept on ringing; and so I shifted my focus to the phone; fucking spark; I didn't mean to crush it; to say I didn't mean to crush him; to say I didn't want to answer the phone; but there was my boyfriend on the line; and there I was with nothing to say; and there he was with nothing: It's late here, It's late here too, What are you doing, Going to sleep, What are you doing, Going to sleep, etc., etc.; and I hung up the phone, and where were we; he had been reading me a story; and he was still holding the book; and he would open the book again; and he would look back at the page; and I thought he would read to me again; but instead he would define a word he thought I didn't know; because he wanted to crush me back; because he did not know I was brilliant; because I did not know I was brilliant; but I knew the word; I knew all the words; I said I knew the word, and he wasn't listening; and when I defined the word, he wasn't listening;

and when he defined the word, I wasn't listening; and when he said something else, I still wasn't listening; and it was then I kicked him in his rib cage; and I actually wasn't joking when I kicked him; and he stood and cast his shadow over me; and I stood in the shadow he cast; and the night still could have gone either way; to say I still could have kept him awake; to say it was then that I started thinking of seduction; no, it was years before that I started thinking of seduction; no, it was at the exact moment of my own conception that I started thinking of seduction; no, it was at the exact moment of my own conception that I was completely seductive; so forgive me for being how I was; forgive me for my performance of female; forgive me for my messed-up desire; I was just a girl and lines were crossed; I was just a girl, and rules were broken; I was just a girl and blank happened once; and blank happened twice; and blank was said; and blank was felt; and blank would be dealt with eventually; and then I would know my brilliance; and the world would know my brilliance; and I would know that brilliance made no difference; because the world was filled with nothing but; because the world was filled with nothing, but; first I was mistaken; first I was lying on my bed; and the phone rang again and I didn't answer; and I turned off the light and thought of sleep; and it was then I saw the keyhole lit up like some kind of too-bright star; and fucking universe; fucking desire; I was falling, again, incredibly hard; and I thought of what you would think of me; and I thought of what you would say to me; and I thought of what you would say of me; and there was the moon scattered across the bedroom; and it was only me and the scattered moon; and it was, hands down, the biggest cliché; it was the biggest perversion, hands down; so punish me for getting out of bed;

punish me for walking to the door; punish me for getting on my knees; punish me for pressing my eye to the keyhole; and punish me for what I saw; and for what I did; and for what I did not; and for all that happened way back when; which was nothing; which was something; like I even fucking know;

UNIVERSAL

I was in this bed that was in no way my bed.

It was like pretty good amateur porn.

It was like the videos my brother got of ugly people fucking.

Nights, as kids, we would watch these videos, me and my brother and his friends, in our basement.

And we would drink what my brother's friends brought to drink.

And we would laugh our heads off at these ugly people doing their fucked-up ugly shit.

It was just like amateur porn.

Because of his soft body I could see the outline of in the dark.

Because of the ugly words he was saying into my hair.

The words were only ugly out of context.

Like if I said them here or on the street.

Like if I said them to a stranger.

Or to your mother.

I should say he was a doctor.

I should say, as well, I was not impressed.

I was only impressed with the smaller details.

Like his eyes, his wrists, the words he used.

And the doctor's kit beneath his bed.

It looked just like you'd think it would look.

It looked like the kits we played with as kids.

There were tools in it that looked like toys.

I was prettier than the girls in the videos.

I was in better shape than the girls, but let's face it.

I was just physically in better shape.

My brother's friends wanted to see me undressed.

They wanted to see me bent like the girls in the videos.

They wanted my legs behind my head, a bored look on my face.

They wanted me drugged and dumb and sweating, and my brother, I know, could have said to them, Stop.

It was my brother who told me about religion.

It was not our religion he told me about.

We had no religion in our house.

He told me about his girlfriend's religion.

It was terrifying, what he told me.

Something about the rapture, and I was terrified.

Something about bodies floating upward into the air.

I didn't believe in the rapture.

Because I didn't believe in religion.

But I could imagine my body floating upward, my head pushing through the ceiling.

I could feel the force that would push my body straight through to the room upstairs.

I should say something here about my father.

But mostly I couldn't get near him.

I mean he was too important to get near.

There was all the important work he did.

There was the study where he did his work.

There was the universe spinning around it.

I was in this bed that was not in any way my bed.

Because I was not good at getting out of things.

It was my biggest flaw that was not a physical flaw.

There was always something that made me stay too long.

Some desire to keep a light lit.

A desire I didn't understand.

And I could ignore what needed to be ignored.

Like his soft body pressing mine into the bed.

Like his girlfriend's things all over the room.

Like my time, my mind.

Like your pride, my brother might have said.

And where is yours, I might have said back.

My brother thought he was better than me.

Just because he met a girl he thought was kind.

Just because he left the house at seventeen.

Just because he left me with my father in the house.

It doesn't matter how I got to his bed.

I mean the specific details don't matter.

We had been to a dinner at someone's house.

I had gotten just too drunk.

And I had pushed myself as far as I could.

I had pushed myself, if you can imagine, to pushing nearly out of myself.

It was all of it too ugly.

Just imagine the ugliest desperation.

Just imagine the bloom just before blooming.

I mean imagine the bloom before one can call it a bloom.

There was a giant tree behind our house.

I could see the tree from my bedroom.

It was not our tree, but the neighbors'.

There was a tree house in the tree.

There were rungs one could climb and a tiny door.

I was not supposed to be in the tree house.

But the neighbors' kids had grown and gone.

And there were bird sounds I liked and there were leaves.

There was the sky getting darker, the sky getting dark.

There was my father calling my name and again.

And the birds calling louder than that.

Our father and mother, before she left, fought brutally.

My mother would stand outside his study screaming.

And I would slam my door, scream, Stop.

And my brother, as well, would scream, Stop.

But my brother's *stop* was directed at my slamming my door and not at my mother and father's fighting.

Then my slamming my door was directed at my brother's screaming, Stop.

Then my mother's screaming was directed at me and my brother.

I did not mean to push as hard, at the dinner, as I did.

But I leaned over the table, took hold of his arm.

Everyone laughed as I wrote my name across his wrist.

Looking back, I have no answer for why I did.

I blame, in part, my drunkenness.

I blame, in part, his wrist.

But these things, of course, weren't really to blame.

Not when you think of what it is to pin blame.

Not when you think of what it is to point at the face of the thing you truly blame.

I liked amateur better than professional.

Amateur had those things you shouldn't see, like broken nails, like messy hair, like fat.

It had people who looked like the ugly couple next door fucking or your parents' ugly friends fucking or your parents.

I liked it because of something having to do with desperation.

The amateurs' desperation becoming mine.

Their rush to get off becoming my rush to get off.

And that fucked-up feeling like the universe was controlled by my wretched gut.

Yesterday, I was standing in line in a store.

There was a woman ahead of me in the line.

The woman was buying a carton of milk.

This has nothing to do with anything.

But the carton of milk was all rung up.

And the woman's money was not in her purse.

And her money was not in her coat.

She said, Hold on, and a man in line behind me sighed.

I could tell what he was thinking.

He was thinking something about this woman.

I was thinking something about her too.

Something about her aloneness.

Something about her desperation, as she dug deeper into her purse.

The man behind me sighed again, and in that moment I hated all men.

I wanted to save this woman from them.

And it occurred to me I had a choice to make, and so I made a choice.

I mean it occurred to me I could buy this woman the carton of milk.

And so I did this very kind thing.

I was in this bed that was someone else's bed.

I wasn't exactly proud to be in it.

I mean I wasn't proud that a part of me was proud.

I felt so proud in certain parts.

And not in the parts literally being fucked.

But more in the parts metaphorically being fucked.

There was this one video we watched the most.

In it the woman's tits were incredibly big.

The guys who fucked her were incredibly big.

The video was so poor quality, it was mostly big parts up close and sound.

The bed had the worst-looking headboard you have ever seen.

It had the worst-looking headboard banging against the worst-looking wall you have ever seen.

It had the girl licking different parts of the guys in a terrible up-and-down way.

And the guys biting down on their lower lips.

The guys squeezing shut their eyes.
The lines they said were just too ugly.
And we laughed our asses off.

One of my brother's friends and I were hooking up as kids.
My brother didn't know about me and his friend.
That I would follow him out when he left.
That we would climb up to the tree house.
That I did whatever he wanted.
Because whatever he wanted was easy.
Because I had a technique that was surefire.
This technique I had took seconds.
It was easy to pretend I was into it.
It was easy to pretend I wasn't pretending.

I bought the woman the carton of milk.
And everyone in the store in that moment was happy.
Everyone in the store in that moment was happy because I had done this very kind thing.
And the woman whose milk I bought squeezed my hand with her terrible-feeling hand.
And as our hands went up and down and up again I thought of how kind a human I was.
I mean I thought of how I had done something kind, something that would somehow advance humankind in its being kind.
And I knew in that moment of no kinder human.
I mean I knew of no human who in that moment would have bought this woman the carton of milk.
And I wanted the clock to stick there forever, to stick in a time where I was kind.
For God to see is what I wanted.

After my brother left the house, my father would call out my name.

It always meant he needed something.

Like something to eat or drink.

And sometimes I would come down from the tree house.

I would make him whatever he needed.

I would leave it outside his study.

But most times I pretended not to hear him.

I could hear only birds, I pretended.

It was just like amateur porn.

Because of his soft body pressing mine into the bed.

Because of the sounds of the bed and his ugly sounds.

He said, What do you want, into my hair.

There were a lot of things I wanted.

Like I wanted to be a kinder person.

And I wanted to know how to do this.

But I said, Nothing.

I said, God.

His girlfriend's things were all over the room.

Her lipstick on the dresser.

Her shirt that looked like a shirt I would like across the back of a chair.

Before she left, we heard our mother screaming late at night.

We heard her banging on my father's study door.

And I would slam my door, scream, Stop.

And my brother would slam his too.

It was unbearable, our limitations.

Unbearable, how we couldn't help.

How we couldn't make her stop.

It could have been love with my brother's friend.

There was something about the tree-house floor.

Something about the sky through trees and the sounds of birds.

I didn't want my brother to know.

Because it said some things about me.

It said I was not the girl his girlfriend was.

His girlfriend would be saved in the rapture.

Her body would float upward into the air.

But it wasn't exactly the body that floated upward.

My brother said it was the soul.

And did I even believe in the soul.

I said, What do you want.

And he said, I want to fuck you.

But he was already fucking me.

So I said, What else do you want.

And he said, Shut up.

He said, Shut the fuck up.

Just fuck me, he said.

My brother's friends wanted me bent like this.

They wanted me spread like this.

They wanted me split like this.

I would say, Take a picture, when they looked at me.

I would say, Fuck you, when they looked too hard.

But they kept on looking.

The woman let go of my hand.

And then the store was just the store again.

The moment was just a moment.

And as the woman was walking out of the store, I felt she was already forgetting me.

And by the time she was out onto the street, I felt she had already forgotten me.

Time was moving forward again, and there was nothing I could do to stop it.

I could only move forward with the time.

That was all anyone could do.

I always stopped laughing when the video took a turn.

When I felt there was something wrong with laughing.

When I felt there was something wrong with me.

Like I was the only one getting off on ugly.

Like I was the only one with a wretched feeling in my gut.

If I were a guy, I would call this story Ugly People Fucking.

And it would be hilarious.

But if I were a girl, I would call it Universal.

And it would be something else.

It would be a dark basement.

It would be old carpet and closed drapes.

It would be the drinks we were not supposed to be drinking.

It would be my father opening the basement door.

And our faces glowing in the light-blue light.

And my father saying something awful.

My father turning off the TV.

My father taking the video upstairs.

It would be me and my brother's friend sneaking off.

It would be climbing the rungs to the tree house.

It would be a dark space that made ugly seem lovely.

It would be the night my brother caught me and his friend in the tree house.

And that was ugly too, my brother standing below the tree as we climbed down.

And it was just too ugly, my brother standing there, waiting there, screaming at me to stop.

There was a time my parents had friends.

They came over for drinks on weekend nights.

They wore low-cut shirts and too-tight pants.

The whole house smelled like smoke and cologne.

My brother and I were sent to bed.

And my mother pretended to be a wife.

And my father pretended to be a man.

I followed the woman up several streets.

This sounds worse, I know, than it was.

I was never going to hurt her.

It was never anything like that.

I don't know exactly what I wanted.

Just the carton of milk, I suppose.

Just to kick the carton of milk out from the grasp of her terrible hand.

I always stopped laughing when the camera moved in on the girl.

Because it moved up close on her face.

And her lipstick was not where it should have been.

And one eye looked larger than the other.

And she looked right into the camera.

My brother and his friends said awful things.

But she kind of looked like someone I knew.

Just someone, and I couldn't laugh.

He was done, and so we were done.

Then he was looking at me like, You really should leave.

But I didn't leave, because I didn't know how.

I was the worst at getting out of things.

He was looking at me like, You really can't stay.

His face looked awful in the light.

His body was just too soft.

He looked at me like, There's the door.

And I stood and walked across the room.

There was his girlfriend's lipstick.

And her shirt across the back of the chair.

I could tell I would really love that shirt.

I thought about taking that shirt.

Not because it was hers.

But because it should have been mine.

But I didn't take the shirt.

I just said something he didn't like.

Then I said something else he didn't like.

I was surprised that he looked surprised.

And it would have been awful, in another context, what I said.

Like if I said it on the street.

Or to your face.

But in this context it was kind.

Earlier, he had pulled the kit out from beneath his bed.

The tools were heavier than you would think.

And I listened to his heart, and I listened to my own.

And I looked into his ears, and I looked into his eyes.

And what I saw in his eyes was not what I expected to see.

I had only expected the color of his eyes, up close.

But when I looked through the tool I screamed.

All I can say is it was terrifying what I saw.

It was lightning across a sky.

It was all of the stars exploding.

It was the biggest fucking mess.

Just imagine the biggest mess you can.

Just imagine the bloom just after blooming.

And yet I looked into his eyes again.

And I looked again into his ears.

And I listened again to his wretched heart.

And I knew there was only so much I could know about others.

And there was only so much others could know about me.

There was nothing religious, I knew then.

There was only this desperate performance.

On the way to his place, we had walked through a park.

We saw a pond in the park I had never, before that, seen.

There was a glow on the pond that I thought, in the moment, was beautiful.

But perhaps I was too drunk to even know what beautiful was.

Or perhaps I was too drunk to know anything but.

I could have followed the woman all the way to her house.

I could have followed her all the way inside.

I could have thrown her down to the floor.

But then who would save her from all of the men.

We sat in the basement in the dark.

My father had taken the video.

We could hear him moving around upstairs.

We didn't know what was going to happen.

We didn't know what would happen to us.

Then my father came back to the basement.

He said, Let's go.

There was a carnival in town.

So he took us to the carnival.

He bought each of us a roll of tickets.

We ate fried things.

We played games.

My father sat reading on a bench.

He looked so strange, sitting outside.

His shirt looked wrong against the sky.

My brother went into the haunted house.

I went on a ride with my brother's friend.

We were locked in this cage together.

He said, Hold on.

Or I said, Hold on.

And the ride started up.

And as we made our way upward, it seemed we were going too high.

And as we went even higher, my brother's friend reached for my hand.

I don't know why it was I screamed.

It's not like he even heard me.

I mean everyone was screaming.

We were suddenly spinning way too fast.

I barely knew my hand from his.

But it was surefire, my technique.
    You want me to say soft hands.
    You want me to say warm mouth.
    You want me to say things into your hair.

You want me to say you're not a mess.
    You want me to say that I'm the mess.
    You want me to say you're not to blame.

You want me to say there is a God.
    You want me to say he's watching you.
    You want me to say he will save your soul.

But what if I say you have no soul.
    What if I say there is no soul.
    What if I say there is only this.
    And what if I'm right.

Acknowledgments

I wish to thank Randall Mann, Chris Kamrath, John Edgar Wideman, Noy Holland, Lynne Layton, Ben Lempert, Gary Clark, John D'Agata, Matt McGowan, Carey Shea, Calvin Parker, Harold Meltzer, Matt Van Brink, Kelley Reese, Patti Horvath, Carole Cebalo, Vincent Guerra, Sebastian Currier, James Hannaham, Evan Wiig, Eileen Fung, D. A. Powell, and Ryan Van Meter.

And special thanks to Fiona McCrae, Steve Woodward, Ethan Nosowsky, Katie Dublinski, Erin Kottke, Marisa Atkinson, United States Artists, the Vermont Studio Center, the MacDowell Colony, the Wurlitzer Foundation, Yaddo, the Blue Mountain Center, the NYU Faculty Resource Network, and the University of San Francisco.

The story "Signifier" alludes to Lacan's and Hegel's thoughts on desire and recognition.

SUSAN STEINBERG is the author of the short story collections *Hydroplane* and *The End of Free Love*. She was the 2010 United States Artists Ziporyn Fellow in Literature. Her stories have appeared in *McSweeney's, Conjunctions,* the *Gettysburg Review, American Short Fiction, Boulevard,* and the *Massachusetts Review,* and she is the recipient of the Pushcart Prize. She has held residencies at the MacDowell Colony, the Vermont Studio Center, the Wurlitzer Foundation, the Blue Mountain Center, Yaddo, and NYU. She has a BFA in painting from the Maryland Institute College of Art and an MFA in English from the University of Massachusetts, Amherst. She teaches at the University of San Francisco.

The text of *Spectacle* is set in Adobe Garamond Pro, drawn by Robert Slimbach and based on type cut by Claude Garamond in the sixteenth century. Composition by BookMobile Design and Digital Publisher Services, Minneapolis, Minnesota. Manufactured by Versa Press on acid-free 30 percent postconsumer wastepaper.